MOMENT OF TRUTH!

"Fire me up, darling," Natasha purred.

Flint took the cigarettes politely, but his smile now was the narrow curve of a hunting shark. He took out his lighter and flicked it to flame. But before the flame reached the two cigarettes at his lips, he exhaled suddenly and blew it out.

"Don't move," he said, pressing Natasha back against the love seat. "Don't move and don't make a sound. . . ."

Is Flint about to make a momentous discovery?
Is Flint about to make a disastrous mistake?
Is Flint about to make love?

DON'T ASK! THERE'S NO TELLING WHAT'S GOING TO HAPPEN WITH A MAN LIKE FLINT.

20TH CENTURY-FOX

Presents

"IN LIKE FLINT"

A SAUL DAVID PRODUCTION

Starring

JAMES COBURN

LEE J. COBB

JEAN HALE

ANDREW DUGGAN

Produced by **SAUL DAVID**

Directed by **GORDON DOUGLAS**

Written by **HAL FIMBERG**

Music by **JERRY GOLDSMITH**

CINEMASCOPE

Color by DeLuxe

IN LIKE FLINT

Bradford Street

BASED ON A SCREENPLAY BY

Hal Fimberg

A DELL BOOK / An Original Novel

Published by
DELL PUBLISHING CO., INC.
750 Third Avenue
New York, N.Y. 10017

First Dell Printing—February, 1967

Printed in U.S.A.

IN
LIKE
FLINT

1

Sunlight on the Virgins, kissing pale sand and coral reef, sunlight turning every vista into a glorious page from a full-color travel folder. Eden, sinless and glowing, with clear light shining bright through the clear, blue-green waters which lap its island shores.

Almost Eden, almost sinless. A swooping gull reaches tree level of the sheltering palms and arcs high again. His beady, suspicious eye has found a house beneath the green fronds. No. More than a house, a whole complex of modern buildings that stretches along the shoreline, then spreads inland. Here the foliage of flowering bushes outlines swimming pools, a series of patios flanks the flashing stream, a penthouse office rises above the palms at one end, and a quaint, rum-and-Coca-Cola-ed bar nestles among the trees.

Shrill-chattering lizards, clambering the stuccoed walls, have a better, more intimate view than the dubious gull. Their cold, reptilian eyes glimpse flesh by the acre: young flesh, old flesh, firm flesh and flabby, wreathed in steam and pummeled by steel-strong hands, caressed and shaped and pressed by plastic rollers, stung by needle-sharp jets of water—hot, then cold, hot again and again icy. Flesh moaning and quivering in the painful ecstasy of beauty's pursuits. . . .

For this complex of buildings in a tropical paradise is Fabulous Face, the foremost shrine of feminine hope in the approximately civilized world, mecca of the unbeautiful who seek improvement, of the beautiful who wish to keep their perfection, of every woman with enough money to afford to go there and worship.

Up and down the corridors of Fabulous Face roved Lisa Norton, creator of the magical retreat and its best testimonial. Slim and vital in her young thirties, Lisa bore, as she walked, a lightsome burden of nearly supernatural beauty. Everywoman's Dream and Everyman's Desire, Lisa's perfectly molded curves were enhanced by pure white hipster slacks and a loosely tied white halter jacket cut to a stimulating V between her proud breasts.

She walked splendidly through treatment rooms and lounges, an ambassadress of ideal charm, with friendly nods for steaming clients, brief words of instruction for the busy members of her staff as they teased hair, beat upon helpless body tissue, pondered the injection of silicone derivatives to brace flabbing female contours.

The great men of the earth usually must die before monuments are raised to them. Lisa Norton, one of the planet's great women, saw her monument alive before her eyes. In fifteen short years Fabulous Face had achieved a reputation that stretched from Saskatchewan to Simla, from Cornwall to Capetown.

She smiled with regal satisfaction as she viewed her creation, but did not slacken the pace at which she walked toward the penthouse administration center atop a circular, exquisitely landscaped knoll.

She inclined her chin in greeting to three clients who sipped on rum coolers at the tree bar. These women were nearing the end of their treatment period. Each with a figure sculptured to its best advantage, the two lush blondes and the lithe brunette wore contour-hugging shorts and the wispiest of bikini bras. The barmaid shared their pleasure at Lisa's passing. Fabulous Face harbored no mere males who might feast their eyes on its end-products.

"What's Miss Norton in such a hurry for?" one blonde wondered.

"Nothing out there but old scenery." The brunette waved a graceful arm at the sea.

"Miss Norton's a very busy woman," the barmaid said with reverent loyalty.

Lisa climbed the long stairway to the penthouse at the same determined pace, still breathing evenly. She made it a point of professional pride to be always in as good condition as the most successful of her clients—and far beyond the physical stodginess of the great majority of males not in Olympic training. The penthouse door, responsive to its electronic controls, swung open when she reached the threshold—open on a vast and efficiently yet delicately designed office area from which Lisa Norton and her handful of associates ruled not merely fashion and cosmetics but every other facet of world femininity.

Decisions made in this futuristic command post affected not only diet, but automobile design, television programming, newspaper and magazine policy, best-seller lists and the layout of shopping centers from Istanbul to Akron, Ohio. Television monitor sets stood in banked rows alongside Movieola machines for viewing (and cutting) feature films. Desks and roomy tables fronted egg-shell bulletin boards collaged with swatches of dress material, drape and carpet fabric and, farther down the line, pertinent newspaper and magazine clippings from worlds as far apart as topological mathematics and children's ABC's.

Lisa smiled at various lady executives, but strode past them to the very end of the penthouse, where four high-power telescopes, mounted on bronze, four-way control unipods, pointed out across the ocean waters. In front of each scope was a severe, comfortable Eames chair and in three of the chairs sat Lisa Norton's three key colleagues: Elizabeth Alden, Helena Robinson and Simone Bellevue. Lisa took the fourth vacant chair without speaking, tuned the telescope controls a hair's breadth and watched with satisfaction her clear view of an enormous rocket firing skyward from its underground silo.

Neither she nor Elizabeth nor Helena nor Simone moved eyes from their 'scopes through the ritualized, scientific pageantry of the launching.

The huge, torpedo-shaped, challengingly male rocket

trembled slowly from its launching pad, seeming almost alive in its shuddering thrust into the air. The four eye-pieces caught every detail in focus as the giant lumbered into its slow initial rise, surging with fresh power from its second bank of rockets, stabbing toward heaven, free and blazingly swift into its computer-appointed path.

"The . . . the color," Helèna sighed, leaning back from her telescope. "The drama! Glorious!"

"Blast-off," Elizabeth said, cool and reflective. "*Blast*-off, a cologne that *sends* you." She wrinkled her forehead into serious thought. "Why not? Might sell. . . ."

Lisa rose from her Eames chair. The other three followed her through the shuttered opening of a sectioned office. Lisa flicked a silent mercury switch, and a king-size color television set built into the wall brightened to life. The Mission Control Room of Agency Z.O.W.I.E. filled the receiver tube with a crowd of U.S. government dignitaries congratulating themselves and one another on the successful launching. The camera panned about the rocketry nerve-center, then let its focus fill the screen with the urbane head of a network commentator.

". . . and everything indicates," the unctuous voice spun through its spiel, "that we're going to get a perfect orbit. Right now we're waiting for the computers to answer the question and then perhaps we'll have an answer from one of the men responsible. . . ."

The camera panned back to the officials and picked out the tame-bear burliness of Lloyd C. Cramden, the nation's top security executive. A uniformed technician, beaming with satisfaction, was pressing a typed message into Cramden's hand.

"Yes, that's it!" The newscaster was back on sound. "We have our announcement. Ladies and gentlemen, Lloyd C. Cramden!"

Cramden's squarish, moustached face seemed to have been designed for projection on television's oblong blur. He twinkled a Foxy Grandpa smile at the watching millions, whose protection from treacherous espionage and nuclear holocaust was his business, and spoke the stiffly ghosted syllables of officialese:

"Ladies and gentlemen, we've done it! The first manned space platform in history is moving into a perfect orbit. But this is just the beginning. In weeks to come other rockets containing weather instruments, cameras, and mapping and surveying equipment will join up with our platform, making it the first true scientific laboratory in outer space. Think of it, ladies and gentlemen!"

The smiles of pride and approval in the penthouse office were as spontaneous and sincere as the same smiles in living rooms and bars and grills from San Francisco to Manhattan.

"We've done it!" Lisa glowed.

Helena opened the panel of a rounded end-table to reveal a tiny, complete bar. She poured champagne for the four of them. They raised glasses in a silent toast as Lloyd Cramden droned on.

". . . and begin a new era of goodwill as this platform passes across all national boundaries and forges new extraterrestrial links in that historic chain which is the Fellowship of Man. . . ."

"Man!" Lisa said, interrupting her toast with a beautiful grimace.

The red telephone at Cramden's elbow emitted a lively, perky un-phonelike doodle-de-doo. The Security Chief finished a paragraph smoothly, then reached to pick up the receiver. The newscaster stepped smoothly on camera as Cramden made a half-turn to speak into the instrument.

"Ladies and gentlemen," the newscaster said in tones of appropriate awe, "that is our President calling Mr. Cramden, no doubt to congratulate him on his part in this magnificent achievement."

In his White House office, President Melvin Muffly cradled his red telephone between chin and shoulder, thus allowing his arms freedom for experimental swings with a number-seven iron while he kept one dutiful eye on the television set. President Muffly had never let his spectacular career be hampered by the false adage that a man cannot do two, or three, things at once.

"Had to call you right now with congratulations, Lloyd," he said warmly to his old friend and colleague. "Couldn't wait for official ribbon pinning. A great job. Now that it's buttoned up, you ought to relax a little. Matter of fact, I thought . . ." The security-conscious Chief Executive glanced about the room and decided to take no chances. "I thought we might have a little round of g-o-l-f, get it?"

"Yes, Mr. President," Lloyd Cramden agreed.

"Grrreat!" said the President. "Tomorrow, Lloyd, sure enough. See you then."

Before Cramden could say "Goodbye," President Muffly had taken a full-swing chop into the soft-pile rug, an official birthday gift from the Shah of Iran, and was looking off into the middle distance with satisfaction.

"Right down the middle," the President said. "Hunnert-fifty yards anyway." Any darn-fool bunch of eggheads could lift a rocket into orbit, but it took a Man to control that tight-packed, pesky white pill of a golf ball.

Oblivious to such high-level byplay, the ladies of Fabulous Face continued to watch the official report. The newscaster had announced the Control Administrator, Colonel David Carter.

"The wild bore!" Elizabeth sniffed at the screen.

"A bore, true," Helena said, "but most necessary to us, no?"

"Colonel Carter," the newscaster repeated heartily. "Right. You must have been an old ball player, Colonel. For a moment back there I thought you were making signals like a third-base coach."

The Colonel gave a slightly self-conscious chuckle.

"This kind of thing?" he said, abruptly signaling *Steal Home* with a handwave to an invisible base runner. "Habit, I guess. And you're right, it does come from managing days too long ago. But this space shot actually, you could say, puts us back in the ball game, doesn't it? I mean, this is quite a day."

Lisa pressed a button beside her chair and let the TV screen shimmer a color crescendo to blankness.

"Puts us back in the ball game!" she mocked, imitating Colonel Carter's hand signal. "Men! But he's right about one thing. This *is* quite a day."

She turned toward Helena, narrowing her fine eyes.

"That is," she said, "it's a fine day if you've really been able to turn out the facsimile model."

"Forgive me, dear, for the day," Helena said, "but I must have my own moment of drama. I'll bring him right in myself."

She crossed the room and stepped through a door at the end away from the general office quarters. Elizabeth and Simone crossed fingers at her back. Lisa knocked knuckles on the rich teakwood of the bar cabinet.

Helena was back in the room within seconds, leading by one hand a tall man whose face and hands were swathed mummy-style in bandages. He nodded to his audience as Helena began to unwrap the gauze coverings of his face.

Lisa could not control the tense drumming on the cabinet top as the familiar visage was gradually revealed.

"My God, he's perfect!" said Elizabeth. Lisa nodded and withdrew her hand from wood. Simone smiled.

"You see?" Helena said. "It could be done. I've created what I promised. The next step, Lisa, is up to you."

"It's all been laid on," Elizabeth said.

Lisa had stepped to the open window and was looking toward the distant skies where the rocket had disappeared.

"Just sit tight up there," she said in a soft, yet commanding voice. "We begin tomorrow. OPERATION DUFFER."

Far above the Virgins, far above Cape Kennedy, far above Washington, D.C., Moscow, London, Paris, the Z.O.W.I.E. space platform coasted gently into a timeless orbit.

Grotesque in the protective coverings of their space suits, two figures made lurching progress toward the sealed door which opened into the space capsule. This would be their initial and cramped home until further hardware was rocketed to fit the platform for gracious living. They went through the door, closing and sealing it behind them against loss of precious oxygen. Then they stepped from the vestibule airlock into the capsule proper.

The first figure slipped off heavy gloves, freeing hands to unlock, unzipper, unlever the helmet fastenings. A hard upward tug released a cascade of golden blonde hair. Then the astronaut tossed the helmet to a bunk.

"This is it, Anastasia," she said in Russian. "What's next?"

Her companion tugged her helmet away from a gamin crop fresh from Fabulous Face's beauty assembly lines.

"OPERATION DUFFER, Sascha," she said. "That's what's next."

2

Halfway through their eighteen holes, President Muffly and Lloyd Cramden paced from the ninth green to tee-off on the dog-leg tenth. Two Secret Service men acted as caddies, and a third, unencumbered by such distractions, rode shotgun (to be more accurate, it was a police positive .38 holstered under his unbuttoned jacket) on the quartet.

The Chief Executive of the greatest democracy in the world was in a high good humor. He had Cramden three down and was bubbling with magnanimous advice.

"Now watch me carefully, Lloyd," he said, teeing his ball on a new sterling tee, the gift of the English Ambassador. "What's wrecking you is you're trying to kill the ball. Brute power isn't the answer, Lloyd. Golf and life have one thing in common . . ." He paused for a moment, wishing Dick Hazlitt were there; this kind of wisdom could dovetail nicely into an informal speech to the N.A.M. "Success is based on timing, Lloyd."

"I've got nine holes to catch up." Cramden huffed as much annoyance as a player might allow himself with his President.

"And you'll go down three more, if you don't shape up." President Muffly chuckled. "Now, Lloyd, I'm going to give you a lesson that will help that swing of yours. Get your stopwatch out."

"Yes, Mr. President." Cramden sighed and withdrew

a slim but accurate chronometer from his trouser pocket.

"I'll tell you when," the President said, taking a series of practice swings before standing up to the ball.

He stepped closer to the ball and addressed it as if it were a convention of World War II veterans.

"Now watch me," he said, "and remember it's all in your timing. Start your watch."

Cramden nodded and pressed a stud on the timer. The President swung into a high backstroke, then froze as one of the Secret Service men called: "Hold it, Mr. President!"

Three guardian hands streaked to gun butts. Over the velvet green came a strange vehicle—a wheelchair being pushed with dangerous gusto by two boys. In the wheelchair sat a shawled, capped ancient.

"It's all right," the President said. "Nothing to be alarmed about."

The Secret Service men kept their hands in position, but some tenseness drained from their stance.

"Whoa, boys!" croaked the wheelchair passenger. "It's President Muffly. My apologies, sir." He nodded to the President.

His horse-power man-power boy-power team dipped their heads in awe and checked the headlong progress of the chair.

"Ask him for his autograph, sons," the old man said.

"Gosh, Mr. President," stammered the first boy, a lock of tousled yellow hair escaping from his cap. "If you'd autograph your golf ball for me, I'll put it right next to my picture of Batman."

"Martin!" the old man rebuked him sharply. "Comparing the President to—"

"Perfectly normal, sir," the President said. "When I was his age the President ran a poor second to Babe Ruth." He took the ball from the tee and scrawled his name with practiced skill on its nubbly surface. He always carried a fiber-tip pen that could write on anything from swimsuits to bread crust. "Go right ahead, son. Let me have your ball, too, Lloyd, for the other nipper."

The first youth had accepted his gift with thanks and courteously put a fresh ball on the tee to replace it. The President signed Cramden's ball and handed it to the other youth.

"Thank you, Mr. President," they said together in the creaking, high accents of breaking adolescence.

"You're very welcome," the President said.

"Now let's not hold up President Muffly any longer," the old man scolded.

The boys took their old positions in back of his chair and, waving back to the twosome, wheeled over the next hillock and out of sight.

"As we were," the President said, stepping back to address the ball. "Time me, Lloyd."

Cramden clicked his stopwatch to a fresh start and the President swung his usual smooth, relaxed swing. The clubhead hit the new ball and a sudden cloud of swiftly dispersed vapor billowed from the crushed membrane that had been disguised as a golf ball. The thin mist seemed to rise instantaneously about President Muffly, Cramden, and all three Secret Service men. And as quickly as it rose, it froze all five to the immobility of statues.

Back over the hillock came the two boys. They burst into view, pushing an empty wheel chair. The elderly patient ran easily ahead of them, pulling away the geriatric rubber mask that had covered his face, revealing the same features that had so delighted Lisa, Elizabeth, Helena and Simone just yesterday at Fabulous Face—features identical, down to the tiny mole at the outer edge of the left eyebrow, to those of the immobilized President Melvin Muffly!

"We have exactly one hundred sixty-eight seconds left," he said to his companions. "Muffly first."

"Yes, Mr. Trent," the first boy answered crisply, and helped his partner lift the stiffened form of the Chief Executive. Then Sebastian Trent, whose retirement from a successful career of acting had flurried Broadway and Hollywood only mildly two years before, waved skyward to direct a large helicopter air taxi to land next to the tenth tee.

The helicopter pilot, a stocky young woman in tee-shirt and dungarees, lent a hand in depositing the President in the plane.

"One hundred seventeen seconds," Trent checked his watch.

The boys collapsed the wheelchair and shoved it into the plane's passenger space next to the President.

Trent rolled up the mask and wadded it into his cap, shrugged out of the loose linen-duster-type coat he had been wearing, and looked into the plane quickly to check his attire against President Muffly's. The pilot, already at the controls, circled thumb and forefinger in an OK signal. Slacks, sweater, shirt, socks, shoes matched perfectly. The boys were in the cabin, one on either side of the President. The pilot touched her controls and the 'copter gave its peculiar, spastic lurch and then lifted into free air.

"Seventy seconds," Trent said to himself, waving the plane away.

He took his time stepping to the tee. He addressed the ball, gave himself a full swing, and connected. The helicopter was already out of sight when Cramden clicked his stopwatch. He watched the ball soar straight down the fairway and bounce to a perfect lie for turning the dogleg.

"Good clout, Mr. President," Lloyd Cramden said.

At the tenth tee the caddying Secret Service men relieved the players of their clubs and started up the cart. The other Secret Service man routinely checked the terrain behind them, then followed. Only Cramden, looking down at his stopwatch with a puzzled frown before he drove, had displayed any astonishment.

"Get it, Lloyd?" the facsimile President asked him.

"Yes, sir," Cramden muttered. He stared down at the watch again.

"All in the timing," President Trent-Muffly said with triumphant self-satisfaction.

Cramden went even further off his game in the last nine holes and the brand-new President took the match by seven holes.

"Buck up, Lloyd." He smiled as they parted at the clubhouse. "Can't win 'em all, you know."

"Thank you, Mr. President," Cramden said automatically, weighing in his mind the prospects of a sleepless night against two blue pills and a foggy morning.

He compromised on one blue pill and four aspirin, but his morning was still as foggy as the nation's worst enemy might desire.

"There's no explanation that fits," he said for the fifth time to Lieutenant Robert Avery, his confidential assistant and good right hand, who sat patiently beside his desk commiserating with his dilemma.

Avery offered a cigar to check Cramden's absent-minded hoist of his pencil to his mouth.

"No thanks." Cramden waved the panatella away sadly. "Gave them up a month ago." He bit on the pencil end with small satisfaction. "If this watch is right—and it's been right in a dozen rocket launchings, right to the split second—then something else is terribly wrong."

"You *could* be mistaken, sir," Avery suggested diplomatically.

"I wish I *wasn't* sure, Avery," Cramden said. "But nothing can alter the fact that three minutes went by that I can't account for. Three minutes in the life of the President. It's not just irregular, it's irrational!"

He worried the end of the pencil between his incisors, tried unsuccessfully to inhale.

"I've put a Top Priority on it," he said, "here and in the key international offices. But nothing turns up that makes any more sense."

An intercom box on his desk flashed white and green. Cramden pressed a lever hopefully.

"Yes?" he barked at the box.

"Grant here," a voice filtered metallically. "Haven't

come up with anything, Mr. Cramden. The truth is, I don't know where to start. An oddball thing like this —I—sir, perhaps Derek Flint would be the man to—"

Cramden switched the lever angrily to OFF.

"Flint!" he said. "That's all I need. With all the resources at our command—"

The intercom blinked again and he depressed the lever.

"Cramden here."

"Ici, DuBois, Monsieur Cramden," came the voice of the famed head of the Deuxième Bureau. *"Je regrette* to inform you our men have reported nozzing. Unofficially, monsieur, I would myself suggest giving this strange problem to Derek Flint. You remember when my own country—"

"Thank you, DuBois. *Merci."* Cramden flicked the intercom lever.

"Flint!" He stared accusingly at Avery as if the whole problem was his fault. "Flint, a maverick. Impetuous. Completely undisciplined, unpredictable, irrational."

"Irrational." Avery picked up the word. "Exactly like the problem, sir."

"You're right, dammit," Cramden said, his jaws at last crunching through the pencil. "Pfglght!" He threw the broken pieces into his wastebasket where the miniaturized radio transmitter planted in the pencil shaft still glowed, still caught every word the Security Chief spoke.

In another wing of the sprawling government complex of offices, Colonel David Carter listened intently as Lloyd Cramden's angry voice came from the small speaker concealed in his desk clock: "Okay, I'll see Flint. Avery, hand me that book on the training and taming of dogs."

Carter pressed an alarm stud to shut off the clock receiver, reached with the other hand for one of his two desk phones. If things continued to work properly, he'd be a three-phone man, maybe four, before you could say K-I-L-L.

"Operator, this is Colonel Carter. I want to place a long-distance call."

The special number switchboard at Fabulous Face routed the call directly to Lisa at penthouse HQ. She listened, a trace of smile lightening her thoughtful face, as Carter relayed his news.

"You were right, Miss Elizabeth," she said, hanging up. "He's turned to Flint for help."

"This masculine loyalty is as predictable as it is childish," Elizabeth said. "Girls, what do you find in the Flint files?"

Helena looked up from the bulky dossier she and Simone had spread out over a tabletop.

"It's quite a collection," she said. "Formidable."

"Yes, yes, of course," Elizabeth said. "His weaknesses?"

Simone held up three color-film transparencies.

"Three of them, it seems," she said.

"Lisa," Elizabeth asked. "The slide viewer, please."

Lisa placed a compact viewer of black-lighted glass on the table and four heads clustered about as Helena placed the slides in position for inspection.

The first had caught a breathtakingly lovely blonde in a moment of poolside relaxation, sunning on a low lounging bench with a minimum of covering. To any male eye the photograph would have brought an automatic reflex of admiration. This was a tougher audience.

"Hairdos like that went out with Toby Wing," Elizabeth sneered.

The second slide did equal justice to an equally beautiful redhead, caught by some hidden camera just between lingerie and full dress.

"Peasant," said Simone, not without a touch of envy.

"Black lace," Helena sniffed. "Wins the vulgarity stakes."

Derek Flint's third weakness, raven-haired and bending over a badminton table in short shorts, fared no better.

"Tacky sandals."

"Dressing to please a *man!*"

"I wouldn't wear it to a masquerade."

Lisa switched off the viewer light.

"A case for Operation Hair Dryer," Elizabeth said, turning to Lisa. "Are you up to recruiting, my dear? After all, Mr. Flint's reputation—"

"I can leave in an hour," Lisa said. "Don't worry."

She was already in Flint's New York apartment when Lloyd Cramden made his arrival in the wide foyer.

Cramden was still clasping the dog book Avery had given him in his office as the elevator doors opened on Flint's first floor.

" 'Avoid tension,' " Cramden read aloud. " 'A dog can sense fear. Show him you're his friend. Offer him food.' "

The two giant Russian wolfhounds at either side of Flint's door lay quiet and stared at the Security Chief with craven impassivity. He walked toward the doorway slowly, drawing from one jacket pocket the paper bag already slightly stained from its toothsome burden of fresh liver.

"Good doggies," Cramden said.

Neither dog moved or even blinked.

With enlarged confidence Cramden reached out and pushed Flint's doorbell.

Before he had removed his hand from the button an outsize German shepherd bitch had come from nowhere in one silent leap. Cramden hastily proffered the bag of liver.

The dog took the bag in its mouth and Cramden's heart resumed beating. But then the dog deposited the bag at his feet and fixed its two rows of long ivory teeth on his hand. The pressure was firm without harshness, but it brooked no argument as the dog tugged Cramden after it through the door and into the living room where Lisa was talking to Flint's three weaknesses.

She had shed the informality of her island attire for a chic but more severe garb, a light suit with an oyster-white blouse and the broad-brimmed hat favored by door-to-door salesladies in the smarter suburbs. She had spread an enticing selection of Fabulous Face beauty products over a coffee table and had presented each of Flint's current staff—Denise, Jan and Terry—with a compact plastic and aluminum Fabulous Face Portable Hair Dryer. She did not permit the entrance of Cramden, right hand still firmly gripped by the police dog, to interfere with her sales pitch.

". . . and at Fabulous Face," she said, "we offer completely individual beauty treatments, styled to a scientific analysis of each personality and taste. For example, if you enjoy a full body massage . . ."

The three girls smiled identically naughty smiles and Denise, the redhead, looked up from the checkbook she was working at.

"I'm sure it's very nice, Miss Norton," Denise said, "but I don't think any of us have to leave town just for a massage."

"Besides," added Jan, the brunette, "I don't think we have the time to spare, do we? I mean, as soon as Derek gets back we all leave for Rio."

"Of course!" blonde Terry sparkled, remembering the plans. "The Carnival! We missed it last year when Derek had to go to Lhasa. We don't want to miss it this time—"

Cramden, trying to remove his hand from the dog's teeth but only inciting the animal to a tighter grip, made a muffled grunt, but nobody paid him mind. Lisa was quickly responding to sales opportunity.

"But that's just perfect," she interrupted Terry. "Our place, Fabulous Face, is in the islands. Just a short flight from Rio. Actually, it's right on your way. Please say you'll come!" She shifted from little-girl winsomeness to woman-to-woman professionalism. "Frankly, it would help me in my job and be grand publicity for

Fabulous Face. Everyone's heard of Mr. Flint and you girls."

"Well, maybe . . ." Jan softened a little. "We can get in some water skiing, get a tan . . ."

"And Derek can pick us up there when he gets back from the desert!" Denise clapped her hands.

"Right!" Jan gave her seal of approval. "Let's tell him."

"Oh, is he here?" Lisa asked, looking around in simulated surprise past Cramden and his canine attendant.

"Why, yes," Terry said kindheartedly. She and her colleagues were used to the magnetic fascination Derek Flint had for all their sisters under feminine skin. "Of course, you'd like to meet him, wouldn't you? I keep forgetting—"

"No, no, that's not necessary." To her disgust, Lisa felt a tingling sensation of blush-warmth climbing from her neck to her cheeks. "Unless—uh—you feel I should. As I said, of course, I've heard of him."

The police dog, by now as bored as Cramden, cleared her throat with a genteel growl.

Terry looked up and gave full notice to dog and captive.

"You're supposed to smile, sir," she told Cramden. "Then she'll let go. The way you're frowning makes her nervous."

"Uh, yes," Cramden said. He forced his lips into a hideous shape that he hoped might pass, to a dog, for jolly good humor. The dog let his hand fall and moved away a few yards, only partially convinced that the Security Chief was not a hired assassin.

"You must be Mr. Cramden?" Terry said. "Right?"

Cramden, rubbing his cramped hand with the other, nodded.

"Well, yes," he said. "I—that is, I don't recall our meeting before."

"No," Terry said. "I only knew you from your picture in Derek's files. We're new, all three of us."

"All of you?" Cramden looked, awed, from Terry to Jan to Denise and back to Terry as all three nodded smiling agreement.

"Derck is out at the pool," Terry said, taking Cramden's arm with a friendly squeeze. "He said to bring you along."

"Excuse us," she called to Lisa, "we won't be a moment."

Jan accompanied Cramden and Terry. Denise, in the routine security procedure that operated smoothly as silk all through Casa Flint, remained with Lisa.

The pool, down a curved corridor decorated with original Rowlandson prints, was enclosed by a glass shell that kept it functional in all weathers. At the pool door, Jan turned away to the library, leaving Terry to finish escorting Cramden. Terry pointed through the door before opening it.

Cramden could see Flint, his muscular, tanned chest bare to the waist, squatting in coarse linen slacks and Rilleau leather sandals by the edge of the hundred-and-fifty-yard pool. Flint had a stethoscope rigged in his ears with its free end dangling into the pool water. Beside him a custom-built Blaupunkt tape recorder sat on the pool wall.

Flint took the recorder microphone and spoke into it with distinct syllabization: "I am hung-ry."

Cramden rapped on the glass of the door loudly enough to make Flint look up from his work. Recognizing Cramden, Flint set down the microphone, took off his stethoscope and turned off the recorder.

In one long, limber stride Flint was at the door, unlocking it for Cramden and Terry.

"Sorry," Flint said. "Can't afford interruption during experiments. Good to see you, sir. Will you have a cigar?" He turned to Terry: "Will you get them for Mr. Cramden? Drawer F-27 in the humidor will be his brand."

"No." Cramden held out a restraining hand to Terry. "No thanks, Flint, young lady. Had to give them up." He looked more carefully at Terry.

"Uh, Flint," he lowered his voice. "What happened to the old—the other girls?"

Flint raised an innocent eyebrow.

"The ones you—uh—had before," Cramden groped for clarity.

"They're married," Flint said.

Cramden scratched his gray thatch.

"Happily, I imagine," he grunted.

Flint raised his other eyebrow.

"I mean," Cramden said, "naturally they were certainly well—"

Flint smiled while the Security Chief groped for a word both correct and polite. Jan had come into the pool area carrying a lab jacket, which she handed to Flint. Terry held it as Flint put it on.

"Naturally," Flint said seriously.

"But didn't you used to have—four of them?" Cramden pursued.

"Right," Flint said, critically checking the hang of his jacket shoulders. "For awhile it was five. *Too much!*" He sighed in pleasurably reminiscent weariness. "I'm trying to cut down."

Cramden was still trying to decide upon the most likely translation of this when, over Flint's shoulder, flashing a dozen feet out of the placid pool water, he saw a large dolphin rise into the air and then fall back into the pool in a rainbow shudder of scattered droplets.

"Hey!" Cramden cried. "Hunh?"

"No chance, Erik," Flint called toward the sleek sea beast. "You've had your lunch."

He wheeled back to face Cramden.

"Now then, sir, what's on your mind?"

"Flint!" Cramden blurted. "That fish out there. You don't talk to—"

"The dolphin is a mammal, sir," Flint said in the gentle, explanatory voice he saved for conversations with small children and executives. "Actually, a member of the cetacean group, or the whale family. Very intelligent animals, sir."

"Whales!" Cramden stifled an eruption of anger and frustration. "Whales, right! What's one more mammal in this household, eh?"

"Oh, he doesn't *live* here, sir," Flint reassured quickly. "He's just staying with us for a few weeks while I finish compiling the dictionary of dolphin sounds. Never been brought properly up to date."

"Dictionary of—" Cramden did splutter this time. He felt like a man who had started off to consult the Delphic Oracle and taken a wrong turn into a Fun House.

"Not words, sir," Flint said patiently. "We communicate by sonic waves. The whole thing is just part of an overall experiment in isomerism."

"Isomerism," Cramden said dutifully. "I see. Isomerism? I don't see."

"Isomerism," Flint said. "The relationship of two or more nuclides with the same mass numbers—"

Cramden was gulping for air, not unlike a grizzly, ancient sea mammal suddenly thrown out of water and into a too thin atmosphere full of nuclides, whatever the hell they were.

"I'm sorry," Flint said mercifully. "If you'll follow me to the library, sir. Jan, would you get the gear ready?"

The dark-haired beauty stepped off briskly ahead of them. Flint linked an arm with the distraught Cramden and guided him back along the corridor.

"Naturally," Flint went on as if Cramden understood even part of his explanation, "though they have the same mass and atomic numbers, they have different energy states and rates of radioactive decay."

"Naturally," Cramden groaned. Flint pushed open the door to his library, a huge room flanked by ceiling-high shelves with a modern billiard table in its center. Cramden stopped at the table and fiddled with the cue ball, letting his eyes rove over the shelves. G. A. Henty's

With Pike and Bike through Holland next to Auerbach's *Mimesis.* The complete set of *The Golden Bough* and the Boy Scout *Handbook.* Morgenstern and Von Neumann on *The Theory of Games* and the Opies' *Oxford Book of Nursery Rhymes.* Mezz Mezzrow's *Strictly the Blues* and *The Cambridge Medieval History* through Volume VII.

Jan pushed a wall button and a section of bookcase swung forward to reveal a whole complex of the most sophisticated electronic equipment, meters, dial indicators, gauges already alive with wavering green lines. The displaced bookshelf had contained a complete set of Trollope, with one stray Ouida—*Under Two Flags*—at the end. It was some kind of nightmare, Cramden told himself.

"Flint, if my problem weren't important," Cramden said aloud, "I wouldn't be here."

Flint was twiddling dials on the electronic shelf.

"It's simply radiant energy transmitted by pressure waves at the speed of sound," he said.

"Most interesting," Cramden said, "but *my* reason for being here—"

"By controlling the frequency of the sound waves," Flint said, "we can produce a musical note. For instance—"

He noted that Cramden was still fiddling with the cue ball. With a faint smile he touched a finger to a protuberance on his belt buckle.

"Flint, this is important!" Cramden snorted.

Flint had removed the tiny tuning fork from his belt and clipped it to the side of his multipurpose cigarette lighter. A careful fingerflick set up vibration in the tuning fork and the room hummed with a faint, high musical tone. The cue ball rolled away in an urgent ellipse from Cramden's fingers.

"Hey!" Cramden said, reaching after it.

"Every element can be destroyed by the proper pitch," Flint said, touching the tuning fork again.

Cramden's hand was less than an inch from retrieving

the cue ball when, with the most miniscule of pops, it disintegrated into a gray-white pile of powder. The room fell back to silence, the musical humming gone.

"Extraordinary!" Cramden admitted.

"A toy," Flint said, readjusting the fork back into the belt buckle.

"And yet," he added, "we are making such strides in the isomerismic field that last year's most advanced text is already out of date."

He picked a book from the shelf before him, looked at its opened pages and shook his head.

"How do you find time to read?" Cramden wanted to know.

"Read?" Flint registered surprise. "I wrote it."

"Walked into that one," Cramden muttered to himself.

"Sir?"

"Flint, dammit, I do have to talk to you privately," Cramden cried out from his heart.

"Of course, sir," Flint said. "Will you excuse us, Jan?"

"Of course, Derek." The dark girl took a second to disconnect some electronic components, and pressed the control to let the shelf swing back into place.

"Now, sir," Flint said when the door had closed behind Jan, "what is it?"

"Flint," Cramden said, sinking into an upholstered leather chair, "something happened while I was playing golf with the President, something totally inexplicable."

"The President?" Flint's ears pricked almost visibly.

"I don't know where to begin," Cramden said, all the confusion of his problem flooding back at once. "It doesn't seem to make sense."

"I'm sure it will," Flint comforted. "We'll put our heads together on it, sir."

"Well," Cramden took a deep breath for a fresh start. "I haven't been playing up to my game lately. Personally, I put it down to too long hours on Z.O. W.I.E. security, but the President felt my timing was off. He asked me to time his swing as an example. With this stopwatch."

Cramden unhooked the watch from his chain and handed it to Flint, who prised open the back of the case as Cramden went on.

"Flint, that swing took him three minutes. You know that's not possible."

Flint had returned the backing to the watch.

"Is it?" Cramden asked.

"No," Flint agreed. "It's interesting, very interesting. The watch itself is in good order. Of course, you've had it checked at the lab?"

Cramden bobbed his head impatiently.

"It's an intriguing problem," Flint thought aloud. "I'd like to look into it, if I may."

"That's what I was hoping," Cramden said. "I'll see that you have all cooperation from all departments. Brought an ID card along with me."

Flint waved away the proffered rectangle of plastic.

"Good," Flint said. "I'll see you in about a week."

"A week?" Cramden protested.

"Is it urgent?" Flint parried.

"I guess not," Cramden admitted. "Every check I've run pans out negative so another week can't make that much difference."

"Fine then." Flint rose from his chair and held out a hand to assist Cramden from the insidious luxury of deep cushioning. "I'll contact you as soon as I return from Death Valley."

"Death Valley?" Cramden grunted, coming to his feet.

"Routine survival test," Flint said. "I run through one a year to keep from getting soft."

Arms linked again, he led Cramden back to the living room, where the girls had resumed their discussion with Lisa.

As Flint and Cramden entered, Jan, Terry and Denise ran to greet their patron. From under the brim of her hat, Lisa took the opportunity to look Flint over carefully. This latest adversary she knew only by reputation; now, on observation, she could judge him to be as potentially dangerous as all his myths declared.

"Derek!" Terry caroled with a wave of one lissome arm toward Lisa. "Miss Norton here has invited us to be her guests at Fabulous Face."

"It's that exclusive health resort in the Virgin Islands," Denise babbled happily.

"It's just a few hours from Rio," Terry said. "I'll check the airline schedules."

She vanished toward the library in a swirl of miniskirt, a twirl of her red pageboy.

Flint threw out his arms in a gesture of mock helplessness, his broad smile warm and sincere. These were not just his girls, they were his family, and their every enthusiasm touched an otherwise unused chord of paternalism deep within him. He knew, naturally, as did anyone exposed to mass-media magazines and newspapers and television, of the wonders of Fabulous Face. He kept to himself a small, inward smile as he wondered whether the resort's notably feminist executives had ever guessed that one of their most cherished skin nutritive creams was based on an antiacid formula discovered some years before by Derek Flint in laboratory doodlings involving a cancer-deterrent possibility. But he would let sleeping dermatology secrets lie; no sense intruding any personal oneupmanship into the girls' obvious and effervescent pleasure.

"And remember," Jan was saying, "that's the week you'll be gone anyway."

Flint pecked a kiss at the top of her head and then stepped to the table where Lisa stood behind her display. He picked up one of the hair dryers and inspected it. Excellent design.

"You're very convincing, Miss Norton," he raised his head to look directly at Lisa. "Your resort must be quite a place."

"Believe me, Mr. Flint," Lisa said. "It is." She could

not resist just a trace of male-baiting and added: "I do hope you'll *allow* your girls to go."

Flint acknowledged the dig with the slightest narrowing of his eyes.

"They don't *need* my approval, Miss Norton," he said. "They want it."

Terry was back with a sheaf of airline schedules. Flint swept all three girls with an avuncular glance.

"You'd like this junket?" he asked.

"Oh, yes!"

"Heavenly!"

"Like a beauty blast!"

"Then why not?" Flint gave his blessing and the three girls clustered at his side with hugs and tender nibbles. Cramden, from his side of the group, shook his head in not quite disapproving wonder. Lisa, from her side, bit her lip at this crude display of female dependency.

"I'll join you in a week." Flint disentangled himself from his staff. "Will you take care of arrangements, Miss Norton?"

"Personally," Lisa said. "As a matter of fact, you girls had better start packing now. We'll leave in a few hours."

The girls fled down the corridor in a colorful scurry.

"Can't thank you enough, Miss Norton." Flint turned back to Cramden as Lisa began to replace her samples in her neat leather case. "Where was I, sir?" Flint said. "Oh yes, the desert. It's not so difficult an operation if you know where to find food."

"Food?" Cramden sniffed. "In Death Valley?"

"All around you," Flint said. "Nature is a bountiful caterer. Snakes, lizards when you find them, but chiefly edible grubs."

"Grub?" Cramden wrinkled his nose.

"Grubs," Flint corrected. "Found in decayed wood, shrubs and under many rocks."

"Grubs?" Cramden was still unconvinced.

Terry, coming in with a tote bag, heard the word

"grubs" and grinned, stopping to listen.

"Grubs," Flint said, "include larvae, pupae. Worms. Anglicized from the Latin *vermiculus*. One of the most edible of foods, still as available as they were in man's centuries before fire and the hunt."

"But how could you eat a grub?" Cramden gulped at the possibility.

"They are succulent, crunchy, a clear white," Flint said with the lilt of a top copywriter launching a new cereal. "The texture and appearance of the best macaroni."

"My tribe lived on them for years," Terry contributed. "Do I look starved?"

Cramden darted a look at Terry's just over five feet of compact, curved pin-up ability. These rosebud lips had gorged on grubs?

"Your tribe?" he asked.

"It was our staple diet," Terry said. "It has a very high protein value and is unusually rich in vitamins and enzyme factors."

Cramden was still staring at her.

"I have since become a naturalized citizen, Mr. Cramden," she said as an exit line.

"I'm sure it's very good." Cramden admitted defeat to the bountifully healthful jiggle of Terry's derriere. "But, Derek, if you'd care for more conventional food, how about dinner with me at Luigi's for a final civilized fling?"

Lisa, snapping to the cover of her sample case, picked up the restaurant name and etched it into her information-storage cells. Things were going to work even more beautifully than she had planned.

"Sorry," Flint said. "I've still got a mess of packing to do. Give my best to Luigi. You might try his vermicelli à la Derek Flint. Something I brought back to him from Ischia last year."

"I'll remember," Cramden said. "I never knew you knew Luigi."

"Helped him out of a bit of a tight spot with the Honored Society," Flint said.

"You mean . . ." Cramden goggled. "The Mafia, Derek?"

"It is considered better form not to use the name," Flint said.

Cramden shook his head as Flint grasped his hand in farewell.

"See you when I get back, sir," Flint said.

He flashed a smile at Lisa.

"And to you, Miss Norton, thanks again."

3

In Luigi's, behind a small door marked merely RESTAURANT in the East Fifties, there are few frills, but the hard core of dedicated customers does not care. The table covers are coarse cloth and the cleanest of them have stains unremovable by the most brutal laundering. The chairs came originally from the mortuary establishment of Luigi's brother-in-law and look it. The ceilings are low and the light is treacherous for reading the spidery handwritten menus in pale purple ink. But the service and the food itself cannot be matched by all the restaurants with gourmet-society scrolls framed on their gilt and ivory walls. People traveled not merely from Seattle to dine at Luigi's; there were some regular customers from Naples itself. One noted film star had it written as a clause into all his contracts that, wherever he had to work on location, he would be flown at least once every two weeks for a meal at Luigi's, but he refused ever to divulge to his producers any more of Luigi's address than Manhattan.

Cramden had come through the familiar door like a parched traveler finding an oasis. After the problem of the stopwatch, after the sex comedy of an afternoon at Flint's duplex, the Security Chief needed the peace and solace that only great food and good wine might bring to a man close to the end of his tether. The martinis had been bone dry, the clams gray-pink perfection. But now Cramden stared down morosely at the plate before him, nibbling at a crust of heavy bread, sipping at the Chianti to get his courage up.

The plate was bountiful, like all Luigi's servings, a

heap of slim vermicelli, ranging from golden where the butter, garlic and Sardinian thyme lay thickest, to a clear, shiny white. Every time Cramden looked hard at the plate, the individual strands of pasta seemed to move faintly, like larva, pupae, whatever the hell Flint had called them, trying to get back under some nearby rock.

Luigi stopped by Cramden's table, looked down chidingly at the untouched feast.

"Something wrong, Mr. Cramden?" he asked. "You haven't touched your main dish."

"Grubs," Cramden tried to explain. "Yeccchhh!"

"Yecccchhh?" Luigi said, offended to the heart. "It's a special dish. Vermicelli à la Derek Flint, no less."

"Sorry," Cramden said, for even five-star generals and security chiefs must grovel before any proper restaurateur. "I'm just not hungry."

"But the chef," Luigi shook his head. "If I bring this back he will not understand."

"Has he ever been to Death Valley?" Cramden inquired.

"I'm not sure," Luigi said, humoring Cramden until the entrance of a new customer took him from the table.

Lisa Norton, in the doorway to Luigi's, was not recognizable either as the genius of Fabulous Face or the saleswoman of the afternoon. She had changed into a wig with a neat bun suitable to the character of vacationing school teacher she had chosen for that evening, but not dowdy. Her garb, although suited, followed her figure, and her skirt, though by no means mini, was generous to her fine legs.

Luigi snapped his fingers and a waiter dashed to Lisa's side to direct her to a table. Somehow it was she who directed waiter and herself to the vacant space next to Cramden.

"Would you care for a cocktail?" the waiter asked.

"A martini, please." Lisa let her accent flatten to a hint of the Midwest. "Very dry."

Cramden, going into his second bottle of Chianti but still terrified by the vermicelli, looked at the woman at the table next to him with bemused half-recognition. For all his espionage training—those endless packs of cards with every facial characteristic!, the magic-lantern flashes with thirty seconds to write a description of a face seen in a tenth of a second!—he did not place Lisa as the saleslady he had encountered in Flint's quarters. But there was something familiar about her, that dangerous ghost of resemblance to someone known somewhere that has landed middle-aged gentlemen in police stations on molestation charges from Beirut to Bayonne.

He took another, deeper swig of wine and stared again.

Lisa awaited her martini, scanned the tabloid-size menu before her. She lifted it closer to her eyes in the dim light and its corner nudged her purse. The purse clattered to the floor, strewing feminine disorder at Cramden's feet.

"Oh, dear!" Lisa cried, bending to retrieve.

"Allow me," Cramden said with heavy courtliness, stooping to help her. His head collided with her bun in a soft bump.

"Thank you," Lisa said. "*So* clumsy of me."

"Not at all," Cramden smirked. The Chianti on top of the earlier martinis had not exactly affected him, but the combination of ingredients plus the sudden stoop to the floor and the bump against Lisa's head combined to give him an agreeable fuzziness. He stood erect between their tables.

"I'm certain it sounds quite familiar," he apologized, "sort of a line, as it were—but haven't we met?"

"I doubt it." Lisa dimpled coyly. "This is my first time in New York. The Big City."

The waiter arrived. He placed Lisa's martini at her place. He noted Cramden's ambivalent position between the tables.

"Would the gentleman care for a drink also?" he asked.

"Well—uh—" Cramden hesitated, shifting his bulk from one foot to the other and back, trying to look respectable in a fatherly way and at the same time dashingly boulevardierish.

"I'm not expecting anyone," Lisa volunteered with a cordial smile. "And that isn't a line either."

"I'd be happy to join you," Cramden said, moving to the chair at her table. An attractive woman and a table that had no trace of grubs. "I'll have a cognac, please. Thomas Hine, Seven Star."

The waiter bowed, cupid's duty done in yoke with Bacchus.

"May I present myself?" Cramden asked. "I'm Lloyd Cramden."

"And I?" Lisa said. "Norma Benson."

She opened her purse and took out a cigarette case, handing two cigarettes to her new escort.

Cramden found himself fumbling both of them in a beefy hand. Recollections of ancient movies about high life and sophistication in the Vienna of Franz Josef stirred in his clogged memory. He put both cigarettes to his lips and poked out his lower lip to cant them upward in what he fondly believed was a cavalier gesture. Lisa proffered a matchbox.

"Light me," she said in a husky voice, hinting who knew what strange delights at the end of the fuse.

Cramden lit a match and it seemed to him that the flame glowed with an unusual brilliance of mingled orange and green and lavender. He inhaled deeply to light both cigarettes and from the first puff the respectable Dr. Jekyll of top echelon Washington, D.C., became a leering Mr. Hyde, a roué loose at a vulnerable age in the wilds of Manhattan.

". . . just this week," Lisa was saying. "My trip here has to be a short one, crowding in everything I can. You see, we schoolteachers are not exactly in the higher income brackets."

Cramden handed Lisa her cigarette and lolled back perilously in his chair with an insouciance worthy of Derek Flint himself.

"I never had a teacher as beautiful as you, Miss Benson," he said, his normal bear's growl tuned to a seductive purr of muted trumpets. "Perhaps it was just as well for what education I absorbed, dear lady. It would have been too distracting to chart colder curves on a sine graph."

"You're quite flattering, Mr. Cramden," Lisa said.

"Truthful would be a better definition," he growled gently, leaning toward her modest yet intriguing cleavage. "Where *do* you teach, Miss Benson?"

"The John Marshall High School, Roanoke, Virginia," Lisa said. "But why speak of me? It's evident that you are a much more important person in a much more important position."

Cramden preened himself. The waiter set down his pony of brandy and discreetly withdrew.

"I'm just one of the many thousands who work for our government," he said.

Lisa crossed one round nyloned knee above the other, careless of where her skirt rode as Cramden ogled unashamedly.

"Wouldn't even have that job," he chuckled lickerishly, "if it weren't for a beautiful taxpayer such as yourself."

He picked up his brandy and raised it in a heroic gesture.

"To the American public-school system," he intoned. "Especially in Roanoke, Virginia."

Lloyd C. Cramden hadn't felt such a hell of a fellow since the first New York weekend he'd taken as a student at Lawrenceville, when the older brother of a classmate—an honest-to-god Princeton sophomore—had introduced him to the old Orpheum Ballroom and a satin-clad, satin-skinned Bronx hostess named Cynthia had made him feel like Prince Charming till his saved allowances of eight weeks were totally depleted.

"To a very charming representative of our government." Lisa returned the toast with her martini. Was there or was there not an answering glint of rakishness in her greenish eyes? Schoolteacher on a holiday, wanting to crowd as much as possible into her short stay in New York. . . .

Cramden's eyes beamed back at her through a thickening film of desire.

"Actually, I'm a professional guide," he said with two-ton coyness. "Available this very evening for a deluxe tour of the city, personal attention included."

"Could I afford it?" Lisa teased.

"There's no charge," Cramden almost snickered, "if the tour proves to be educational."

He could hardly believe that such a glib flow of what he considered to be Noel Coward dialog was coming from a throat used only to the dry specifics of security briefings. Noel Coward would not have believed it either.

"I'd be delighted, Mr. Cramden." Lisa struck at his bait. "Now, whom shall we really toast?"

"You name it," Cramden said, withholding an impulse to add "Baby-doll" as somehow dated in 1967.

"Here's to the team," Lisa said with a safe irony that Cramden could never have been expected to penetrate. "To our man in the White House!"

Even in his state of mixed muddle and euphoria something came home to Cramden. There had been a golf match and three minutes had been lost. . . .

But Lisa was looking up at him with pouting lips and he stopped struggling.

"I'll drink to that," he said, patting the uppermost knee. "To our man in the White House."

Lisa let him pat, let her head incline toward his shoulder, let him taste those pouted lips with a brushing kiss.

A grandiosely overtipped waiter found them a cab five minutes later and Lisa gave the driver the destination. Cramden, for all his initial amorosity, dozed against her all through the drive.

"Need any help, lady?" the cabby asked when he stopped in front of an apartment that had known better and more respectable days.

"I'll manage," Lisa said, propping Cramden up against her side.

She let the cab go around the corner. Then, with

judo-steeled muscles, she hefted Cramden over one shapely shoulder, carried him into the building, and took the elevator to the tawdry room kept by the organization against just such eventualities.

Ungently, she stripped Cramden of his jacket, shirt and trousers, shoes and tie. She tumbled the body in shorts and singlet onto the rumpled bed and retired to the bathroom for her own preparations, removing her wig with delicate care.

When she came out of the bathroom, sleazy in a none too clean slip, Cramden was snoring horrendously.

"Pig!" she said, Circe disguised as a slattern, and went to the window fronting the street to raise and lower the blind twice.

Then she sat down on the side of the bed next to Cramden and waited.

It was not a long wait, only half a cigarette, before an officious tattoo on the door was followed by a slamming rush that wrenched it open.

Colonel David Carter of Z.O.W.I.E., accompanied by agents Austin and Cooper, hurtled into the sordid bedroom. Lisa, alerted by the first door tap, was leaning over the comatose, unshaven Cramden in a disheveled, Hogarthian embrace.

Cooper unlimbered his Hasselblad camera and took a quick series of strobe shots from several unflattering angles. Colonel Carter, his features stolid and stern in the execution of duty, shook his chief by the shoulders. The combination of strobe flashes and Carter's shaking brought Lloyd Cramden back from dreams of prep-school dissipation to the cold, real world.

"Arrrghh!" he said. "Grrrmmmpph!"

"I'm sure you can explain all this, sir?" Carter said respectfully.

"Explain?" Cramden sat up in the bed. He groped for trousers that weren't there. He looked wildly about from the strange, lipstick-smeared harridan at his side to the stained walls.

"How did I get here?" he asked angrily.

"That I don't know, sir," Colonel Carter said. "Perhaps you'd better get dressed, sir."

Cramden lurched from the bed and stood up. The utterly alien woman, no possible kin to anyone Cramden could remember, put an arm around his waist.

"Don't run off, honey," she said.

Cooper let go another strobe shot.

"Hey, Major, don't do that!" Cramden said, shielding his eyes from the light.

"Sorry, sir," Cooper said. "Just obeying orders."

He checked his focus and took another shot.

Cramden turned on the woman next to him, took in more fully her brittle orange-yellow hair, dusty black at its roots (a labor of ludicrous love for the skilled wigmakers of Fabulous Face), her eyes smeared with congealed mascara, a hell-reek of cheap wine on her breath.

"Who are you?" Cramden asked. "Where did I meet you?"

Lisa kept her face in shadow for extra insurance.

"Don't be mean, honey," she whined. "Just because I'm not made up now. We had a good time, din' we?"

"Get in the bathroom, you," Carter ordered with disgust. "I want to talk to Mr. Cramden alone."

"Awright," Lisa said. "But I got some rights. You try any rough stuff with me, Assistant Commissioner Benghazi's gonna hear about it."

"Made up!" Cramden choked, following her retirement to the bath. "I never *saw* her before!"

"I'm sure you can explain it, sir," Colonel Carter said smoothly. "But I will have to take you into custody for now. Your own regulation, sir. I'll arrange for an audience with the President in the morning. Any decision will be made by him."

Cramden nodded understanding. He *had* made the rules. Any official of Z.O.W.I.E. had to be above suspicion, just or unjust. Cold, hard rules for a hard, cold war. And they could not be suspended for anybody, least of all himself.

"Austin," Colonel Carter directed. "You and Major

Cooper take Mr. Cramden to the car. I'll stay and question the woman."

Cramden was approximately dressed by now. He did not bother to knot his tie, a matter of trivia in present circumstances. A good soldier even in disgrace, he followed Austin through the door, Cooper guarding his rear.

Colonel Carter listened for the sound of the descending elevator and then called toward the bathroom: "Ready, Miss?"

Lisa Norton stepped out of the bathroom. Once again she was a proper schoolteacher from Roanoke, Va.

"Congratulations!" Colonel Carter exclaimed. "Still a lot of life in the old—"

"Spare me the familiarities, General."

"General?" Carter wavered before Lisa's icy stare.

"You did a good job," Lisa said. "You're about to be promoted. We take care of our own, General."

Carter beamed.

"Just remember," Lisa said. "You'll be stepping into Cramden's shoes. See that they fit. Now I have things to attend to. You may go."

"Yes, Miss Norton!" Carter accepted dismissal with military obedience. He did an about-face and left the room.

The meeting in President Muffly's office in the White House was an ordeal Lloyd Cramden had never anticipated when he had embarked on a career of public service almost two score years before. Yet he had to admit that the President was not unkind. It all boiled down to a set of seemingly undeniable facts that both he and the President had to face. He could not even blame Carter, a punctilious and hard-working officer he had brought up in the Z.O.W.I.E. organization himself.

"You met this woman for the first time," President Trent-Muffly went over the report sheets in front of him once again. "You had a drink with her, and you can't recall anything afterwards?"

"I can only assume that the drink was drugged," Cramden repeated with a tired shrug.

"What does your breakdown show, General Carter?" the "acting" President asked.

Carter studied a typewritten sheaf of papers.

" 'Luigi, the proprietor of the restaurant, didn't get a good look at the woman,' " he read. " 'As to the glasses they drank from, laboratory reports show no trace of any known drug.' "

The President looked sadly at Cramden.

"The schoolteacher lead?" he asked Carter.

"No trace there either, sir," Carter said.

"It was the John Marshall High School in Roanoke, Virginia," Cramden said.

"*That* is interesting," Carter noted. "The school had been vacated and the students merged into a newer and larger school quite a few years ago. But more important, sir, is the evidence from the choice of this school, of a breach of security."

"Go on, General," Trent-Muffly prompted.

"The old school site supposedly is presently Top Secret," Carter said. "A training center for Special Forces Project, Green Beret."

The President whistled incredulity and unhappiness in one thin, fluted note. He had been a great actor; he still was.

"You can shed no light on this, Lloyd?" he asked.

"No, sir." Cramden wriggled in his seat like a schoolboy in his headmaster's office.

"And the woman in the hotel, Carter?" the President asked.

"Skid Row chippie, sir," Carter said. He looked apologetically to his recent chief. "I'm sorry, Mr. Cramden."

The President spun his chair to gaze for a moment through the curved window.

"I'm sorry, Lloyd," he said, spinning back to face Cramden. "Nobody knows better than I what a faithful servant you've been to me and to this country we both love so dearly. I'm sure you will be vindicated at your hearing. Until then, necessarily, you're under suspension. However, you can continue to use your office and to have the assistance of Lieutenant Avery. We'll try to keep this out of the papers—if it isn't too late. You can be sure of one thing, though, Lloyd. I'll never turn my back on you."

He spun the chair again, facing Carter, his back to Cramden.

"Now, General," he said briskly, "we had better discuss some of the key security problems now in your hands."

Cramden had too much pride to wait on a more formal dismissal. Without disturbing Carter or the President by a spoken farewell he walked quietly from the White House office.

He directed the chauffeur of his official limousine to drive him aimlessly about Washington for over an hour before he went to his own office. No knowing how long he'd be left the courtesy of the limousine and he had had, in the past years, too little time to let his eyes enjoy the monuments of the nation whose security had rested in his hands. The Washington Monument, its piercing skyward thrust seeming to herald the rocketry undreamed of when it had been built. The classic harmony of the Jefferson Memorial, a tribute to the far-ranging mind of the man who had created the moral and intellectual base of the Republic, whose capital honored him. And the Lincoln Memorial, which now came close to bringing moisture to Cramden's eyes. These three men and all that they stood for. And he, their honest and devoted servant, wearing the stain of disgrace. . . .

He let the car take him to his office, where good old Avery, the one man left to him, waited.

Avery waited behind a desk cluttered with the morning papers. *The Wall Street Journal* was the only one which did not feature a photograph of the trouserless ex-Security Chief and his dubious lady companion on the front page.

Cramden forced himself to glance through every paper.

"Newspapers, television, radio," Avery groaned. "Who could have leaked it to the press, sir?"

"What difference does that make?" Cramden asked dully. "Over thirty-five years in the service. Tunis, San Juan, Caracas, Burma, and now this."

"Sir, a man is innocent until proven guilty."

"These headlines don't agree with you, Avery," Cramden said. "Don't you realize that I'm ruined! Disgraced!"

"Your hearing is only thirty days away," Avery said. "You're certain to be cleared."

"Who reads retractions?" Cramden said bitterly.

"Sir, this is more serious even than those missing three minutes," Avery flared. "I'm positive Flint could—"

"Flint?" Cramden snorted scorn. "He'd have a field day at my expense."

"She *was* ugly, sir." Avery clucked sadly at the newspaper photograph.

"Forget about Flint," Cramden sighed. "He'll be leaving for Death Valley very shortly anyway."

Avery had never known his chief to give in without a fight. He could remember times of his own disgust and weariness when the Old Man had pumped new life into him. Now was the moment to return the favors.

"In that case, sir," Avery said briskly, "we have no time to lose. May I have your permission to act, sir?"

Cramden gave a shrug of agreement, and Avery, picking up one of the most offensive tabloids, raced from the room before any change of mind could stop him.

He chartered a jet at a private airfield and, once airborne, got a cross-bearing on the private Lear Jet that had just left New York carrying Derek Flint to his survival test.

"We'll be flying almost parallel," Avery told his pilot. "Intercept approaching Death Valley and hold for my signal."

He used the rest of the trip to finish reading two

paperbacks he had bought at the airport.

Coming into Death Valley, Avery could see Flint's sleek Lear slowing a little ahead of them and below.

"Overtake," he instructed the pilot, "and hold even."

He strapped on his parachute and stood, braced by a guyline, at the open door in the plane's side.

As soon as he saw Flint emerge from the Lear he let himself fall free. He did not pull at his ripcord until he was even with Flint.

Flint's chute blossomed at the same moment.

"Why, hello, Lieutenant Avery." Flint was polite even in midair. "Something up?"

"This," Avery shouted, holding out the tabloid folded as firmly as possible against the winds.

" 'CRAMDEN LOSES ZOWIE HEAD JOB,' " Flint read and then looked down at the photo of Cramden and Lisa.

"Yeccccch!" Flint said, waving a hand signal to his Lear.

Flint's pilot banked, turned and came back beneath Flint and Avery and Flint spoke his orders into a throat mike.

"We'll be back in time to see him today," Flint assured Avery in the comfort of the Lear Jet cabin. "You can put through a call from here."

Thus Cramden was waiting for them when they arrived at his office, wearing a worried rut in the pile of his executive carpeting.

He stopped his pacing with relief and greeted Derek and Avery with the cordiality of a lost child rescued by friendly policemen.

"Sorry I've interrupted your Death Valley jaunt, Derek," he said, and handed Flint the transcript of charges, made up in triplicate and forwarded from General Carter's HQ.

"Nothing, sir," Flint reassured him. "My survival test is a minor matter compared to *your* actual survival as Security Chief. We've had differences in the past, sir—mostly matters of procedure—but I've always slept a little better at night knowing you were on the job."

This exchange ended the courtesies of protocol. Flint studied the charge sheet, threw a pertinent question now and then at the waiting Cramden and Avery.

"And that's all you remember, sir?" Flint said at last.

"I've been going through my mind ever since I woke in that room," Cramden said, "and that's everything that's in it. I can assure you that that painted crone was no woman I'd ever seen before, much less anyone I'd have been interested in—uh—knowing better."

"So much the conscious mind can tell us," Flint said. "Sometimes the unconscious is more revealing." He touched his wristwatch and a thin circle of light glowed from its edge. "Sometimes we find far down in the mind areas of desire mercifully concealed in our waking hours—"

"Damn it, Flint," Cramden grated through frayed nerves. "You know I'm no Don Juan."

Flint smiled faintly, holding the watch unobtrusively in Cramden's field of vision. The bright lighted circle rotated slowly.

"I'm sure of that, sir," Flint said. "The question is: Since raw animal passion is ruled out, what was the *woman's* motive?"

Cramden tried to look indignant but looked merely wounded.

Flint moved his watch elbow slightly in a careful rhythm.

"Raw animal . . ." Cramden mused. "Well, see here now, Flint . . ."

Avery's eyes, too, had begun to follow the twirling circle of light.

"It *is* ruled out, I assume?" Flint spoke softly.

"Yes," Cramden said, his speech heavier. "I just meant—of course it's ruled out. You should have seen her with no makeup on."

"Take your time, sir," Flint's cadence was a lullaby. "I'm sure it was a traumatic experience."

Cramden's eyelids drooped and fell shut. Avery blinkily followed the same pattern.

"You are in Luigi's," Flint intoned.

"Luigi's," Cramden repeated, shuddering in hypnotic sleep. "She dropped her purse. I assisted her. We introduced ourselves, and then . . ."

Cramden groped into the air before him and Flint, thinking quickly, held out a pack of cigarettes.

"And then . . ." Cramden picked at the pack and removed two cigarettes. Flint grinned at the exaggeratedly romantic gesture with which Cramden placed both cylinders in his mouth. He held out a box of matches and Cramden took them and lit the cigarettes, held one gracefully forward to an imaginary beautiful schoolteacher from Roanoke, Va. Flint took it in midair.

Eyes still closed, Cramden's face twitched from its usual sobriety to a lecherous leer.

"That's it," Flint said to himself. He pressed the watch control and the light blinked out. A snap of his fingers and Cramden, leer erased, was opening his eyes, Avery fidgeting awake on the chair beside him.

"Cigarettes, matches," Flint said.

"What about them?" Cramden asked, rubbing his eyes.

"Of course." Flint still communed with his own thoughts. "I should have guessed."

"Guessed what?" Cramden demanded.

Flint had his lighter out on the desk. He was sliding a side panel to remove a tiny pair of scissors.

"Would you hold steady just a moment, sir?" he asked.

As Cramden held a motionless pose, Flint clipped one short length of hair from his moustache.

"Paper, please?" Flint ordered Avery.

Avery slid a stenographic pad across the desk and Flint deposited the hair at its center.

He took a fountain pen from his inside jacket pocket and, under the curious eyes of Cramden and Avery, touched its clip to release a thin rod with a circle looped at one end. He lowered his head toward the paper and blinked his left eye. A tiny contact lens dropped on the corner of the pad.

Flint manipulated the fountain-pen rod so that the lens was seated in the looped end. Then, flicking on a light source in the pen, he studied the filament from Cramden's moustache.

"Interesting," he said, straightening up. "Singed, of course."

Cramden and Avery were as mesmerized by Flint's action as they had been by the watch light.

Flint raised the paper to his face and sniffed at it thoughtfully.

"Hmnn," he hummed. "Styrax, ilang-ilang, mimosa, hyacinth, cananga." He looked up into two inquiring faces.

"A combination of rare herbs, exotic flowers and certain oils," he explained, sniffing the paper again.

". . . and Macedonian brawley," he said happily. "Combined, of course, with the ash, the residue, euphoric acid as the primary agent."

He put the pad down, returned the contact lens to his eye and pushed the rod extension back into the body of the fountain pen.

"I think that takes care of it," he said.

"What?" Avery goggled.

"Euphoric acid?" Cramden questioned.

"Centuries old," Flint said. "Discovered, according to cuneiform records, by the Assyrians during the reign of Hammurabi. Any date, of course, can be only an approximation."

"But what is it?" Cramden prodded impatiently.

"A psychic deinhibitor," Flint explained. "A tranquilizer which conversely stimulates one's libido while giving a feeling of reckless and sexual euphoria. Combined with alcohol it becomes a quick-acting soporific. Roughly, one could say it bears the same relationship to LSD as LSD does to aspirin. Decidedly dangerous in the wrong hands."

"Nonsense," Cramden blurted. "I recall having a drink. Obviously drugged."

"The lab reported, sir," Avery reminded him, "no trace of a drug in the glasses."

"Administered through the cigarettes, from the ignition of the match," Flint said, "there would be no possibility of traces reaching the glasses. In any case, euphoric acid mixed with alcohol leaves no residuary evidence."

"All right," Cramden said. "I'll buy it."

"But, like most solutions," Flint said soberly, "this one raises a fresh problem. You see, sir, euphoric acid does loosen the tongue. Is there, was there anything of importance you might have revealed before passing—falling asleep? Or in your sleep?"

Cramden, misery etching his grizzly bear features, looked from Avery to Flint.

"I just don't know," he said. "All I do know is that there's something going on, Flint. Something threatening and too close for comfort. It could be in my own organization. But how can I find out when Z.O.W.I.E. itself is off-limits to me?"

". . . off-limits to me?" the clock speaker in General Carter's office, linked to an ever-replenished supply of pencil transmitters, broadcast the words clearly.

"Damn' tootin' off-limits!" Carter grinned, his own best audience. "And that's how it's going to stay in this ball game."

"But not to me, sir," he heard Flint's voice, calm and meaningful.

"The great Derek Flint." Carter sneered at the speaker dial. "Grandstanding as usual."

"Flint, we're talking about a Top Security complex." The querulous officialese in Cramden's voice came through the speaker as if he were in the empty chair next to Carter. "If you should get caught, there's no way to protect you. My teeth have been drawn, Derek. It's too risky."

Carter's lips drew back in the smile of an alligator watching a schoolbus crossing a rickety wooden bridge in the Everglades. He scribbled boyishly on the desk pad at his elbow. FLINT appeared in block capitals and then, beneath it, a crude skull and crossbones with R.I.P.

Rest In Pieces, if he tangles with the disintegrator assembly, Carter thought cheerfully.

"But Z.O.W.I.E. must be opened up for inspection," Flint was saying.

"It's all out of my hands now," Cramden sighed.

"Then I'll look into the matter tonight, sir." Flint's reply was sharp and clear.

The clock dial picked up the scraping of chairs and the shock-absorbed slam of Cramden's office door.

"Best idea the girls ever had, letting Cramden keep his old roost," Carter chuckled to himself as he turned off the receiver.

He pressed one of his intercom buttons and, when the light flashed, spoke into it.

"Major Cooper?" he said. "I believe we may expect a visit from Mr. Flint tonight in the security area. Set up a gala reception for our hero. Right!"

He turned off the intercom and leaned back. The smile was broad; the alligator could see the rickety bridge actually swaying.

4

The central Security Area of Z.O.W.I.E. was an organized masterpiece of impenetrability. Trained manpower and the most subtle devices contrived by man's science worked hand in glove, cog in gear, transistor in beam to insure that neither Russian, Red Chinese nor even carelessly bumbling one hundred-percent American might pass its threshold without proper authorization.

Here were housed not only a handful of specialized and extrasensitive offices—cryptology, war games, computer central—but the banks of microphotographed and encoded records that recorded every "bit" of information that Z.O.W.I.E. agents had gathered from Turkey to Siberia, Mukden to Peking, in the years of the Top Secret agency's existence. Here, beside the notated preference of a certain Central American politician for platinum blonde girls wearing high-button shoes nestled the fact that Staff Sergeant Elmer Brewster had once, six years ago on Okinawa, sold a PX roll of color film on the Black Market. The few crammed acres were a repository of all varieties of data, a national and international conscience and encyclopedia.

Here also stood in all its science-fiction majesty the Z.O.W.I.E. Disintegrator, a nuclear furnace that could reduce to thin ash anything from a prototype tank to an onion-skin carbon of an official document after microfilming. No rubbish collections for Z.O.W.I.E. Every wastebasket, from the most innocent stenographic pool and from the most sensitive encoding office, found its way—pre-shredded as an added safety factor—to this thermal monster which blasted it, hell-hot, to atomized particles of irreducible dust.

By night there was only one entrance. An armed guard stood at the door, checking through its small, bulletproof glass window, every arrival, every exit.

A sergeant at the head of a squad of maintenance men, flanked by a guard armed with a machine carbine and wheeling hand trucks holding the day's collection of dispensable documents, came abreast of the door.

The door guard nodded recognition, slid a tray out from under the window, and waited for the sergeant to insert his computer-coded identity card. The electronic scanner approved the card, the guard pressed his entry button, and the gate swung open.

As the gate opened, a red light flashed to alert interior guards and a hooting klaxon sounded until the maintenance squad had entered completely and the door closed behind them.

The squad members, uniformally robotized in gray Eisenhower jackets, "MAINTENANCE" stitched boldly on each back, tipped their carts into the disintegrator's opening mouth. Inside that mouth, merciless fangs of tool steel masticated their evening meal before consigning it to nuclear heat.

Trucks emptied, the squad trundled the empties back to the gate. The guard, counting the number carefully to check against the admission figure, opened the gate to let them out. They filed out to the raucous klaxon hoot, which died when the gate shut behind them. The squad turned right except for its last member.

Derek Flint turned left and shoved his truck under the shadow of a ventilator shaft. He took off his jacket and turned it inside out. When he put it back on, it was still an Eisenhower jacket, but a tailored officer's model, complete with ribbons, division patch, regimental badges, and the eagles of a full colonel on its shoulders. He pulled a flat pancake object from a trouser pocket, banged in against his knee. It popped out into an officer's garrison cap, braided handsomely in gold.

With the stiff gait of a West Pointer, Flint strode back from the shadow and up to the gate. The guard peered out and Flint, having noted that the guard left all signature examination to the electronic device, felt safe in inserting on the tray the plastic card he had picked from the squad sergeant's pocket.

The electronic guardian gave him its blessing. Lights and klaxon performed spendidly as he was allowed inside the gate.

"Now, I'll need your mission identification papers, Colonel," the guard requested.

"Of course," Flint said. He took out his wallet and handed it to the guard.

The guard bent his head to look. One karate chop put him out of action.

Flint retrieved the wallet with its ID card dating back to a long-ago assignment from Cramden.

"It wan't a good likeness anyway," he said to the unconscious guard.

He crossed the disintegrator area and entered the core Z.O.W.I.E. computer center. At this hour, science stood alone on guard over the building; it was assumed that the gate guard supplied sufficient human control of entry to the grounds.

From the foyer, Flint looked down the long hallway and saw the lighted, clinically clean room at the end that housed computer and recording banks dealing with Z.O.W.I.E. space projects. Here was at least some of the data he had to verify to confirm the slight but nagging hunch that had been building in his mind since he had first combined the problem of the missing three minutes with the badger game framing of Cramden.

He took his all-purpose lighter from a pocket and turned a screw so that a miniature viewfinder, a baby's-fingernail-size screen of pale blue, blossomed from the lighter top. He fixed his eye to the spectographically sensitive material and sighted down the hallway.

What had been to the naked eye a bare corridor now, through the specially sensitized viewer, became a barred corridor. Horizontal infrared beams, spaced a foot apart, ran from ceiling to floor.

Flint smiled. Another man's mind, in this situation, might have been occupied with degrees of measurement, possible methods of electronic blockage. Flint was happy remembering a lilting Spanish-Caribbean tune.

He retracted the view finder and replaced the lighter in his pocket. Then, humming gently to himself, he advanced toward the center of the corridor with a lurching, rhythmical gait.

"When a banana drop from de tree," he sung softly,

"Always dat banana falls on me.

"If a barracuda think he bites some skin,

"Always my leg dat barracud' teeth in."

Scant feet from the point where the infrared rays crossed, he arched his body backwards and, without missing a beat of rhythm, let himself sink to where his head almost touched the ground. Then, in perfect limbo form, he propelled himself underneath the lowermost beam with less than an inch to spare.

"Tourista throw de money, native boy dive," he sang.

"Money sink to bottom before ever I arrive."

His head, garrison cap and all, had passed the barrier. He straightened to his full, lean height, brushing his hands against his trouser legs.

"So far, so good," he said, abandoning the limbo beat.

He took a few seconds in the computer room to orient himself. It had been several years since he had been in this section—on the problem of the missing isotope—and it had changed and expanded. But Flint was familiar with the labeling symbols currently in use in Z.O.W.I.E. and he had known before entering what data he wished to study.

The Gamma machine would be following the newly launched space platform. He located the squat, gray enameled box and examined its controls. This should be the one.

In response to Flint's pressure the machine hummed,

gave a subdued series of polite clicks, and obligingly disgorged a two-foot tape of computer symbols.

His eyes became slits of concentration as he deciphered the messages on the tape. It told of a successful launching and a mission going well, but there were small items that prickled Flint's suspicions, not so much actual discrepancies as infinitesimal mathematical nudges.

He took out his lighter again and ran some quick calculations on the almost microscopic slide rule that issued from its base. He did them over again and shook his head, putting back the slide rule as he moved to the next machine, an electrocardiograph transmitter linked directly to the space-platform astronauts. This could be the ultimate revelation.

He pulled the band from his wristwatch, counting the numbers etched on each link as he observed the two stylographs of the cardiac recorder tracing their thin red lines across an unrolling bluish plateau of graph paper.

These were healthy hearts operating at comfortable and unstrained efficiency. No sudden peaks or lows, a jagged line keeping an even boundary along its unwinding length.

Nothing there, but the frequency . . .

Flint referred again both to watch band and to the sweeping second-hand.

"Eighty on the button," he said with a thin grimace. "Very interesting!"

He let the watch band snap back. He had no need for notes. The fresh information went into his own storage banks, the crammed and ever-accessible cells of Flint's disciplined brain.

"What could he pick up on the cardiac machine?" General Carter, observing through a peephole panel far above, asked Major Cooper.

"With Flint, who knows?" Cooper shrugged. "We've got him in a good spot to knock him off, sir. Why wait?"

"Right!" Carter whispered. The observation room was pitch dark lest light leakage betray its presence to anyone in the computer area below. It had been added and perfected only months before.

General Carter pressed the top of a penlight flash and gave three blinks, the agreed Assault Alert signal, into the blackness behind him. Waiting strongarm members of Z.O.W.I.E.'s élite combat guard corps signaled back with flashes of acknowledgement.

It was a giant mousetrap with the computers and their precious information as bait, Flint for victim.

And Flint, innocent and ignorant of the hazard, walked unhurriedly down the computer line, idly observing different dials, poring over tapes and teletype sheets.

"Ready?" General Carter asked Major Cooper.

"All the boys have answered," Cooper said. "Should be in position to strike."

"Okay," Carter said. "Three, two, one, zero!"

He pulled a switch at the side of the observation room. Suddenly the whole area below, the soft dimness where Flint stood, was flooded with piercingly bright light. Three men darted from a concealed doorway near the foyer and cut off the corridor. Others swarmed down emergency stairways at either end of the computer banks.

Carter flipped open the blinds which had screened his observation post. Through a wide panel of bullet-proof glass he could see every movement on the bright expanse of floor below. Flint stood motionless, hands loose at his sides.

General Carter selected a lever from the lighting and alarm board and filled the building with the ominous brazen hooting of the klaxon. Anything extra to burden Flint's nervous system would help.

Two blocks away, Lloyd Cramden still sat at his desk, poring over papers, trying by sheer willpower to make some breakthrough.

"It's late, sir," Avery pleaded with him. "I think you should go home."

"I've got to find a way out of this mess," Cramden muttered.

"After all, sir," Avery said, "the hearing isn't for a month yet."

"I'm not even thinking about that, Avery," Cramden said. "I'm thinking about Flint. I may have gotten him into something terrible this time."

"Sir, no one gets Flint into anything," Avery reasoned. "Not against his wishes."

"That's true," Cramden admitted, "and yet I feel the basic responsibility. I may have been called stuffy, but nobody could say I'm a buck-passer. . . . What's that?"

The raucous, jeering note of the full Z.O.W.I.E. alarm system, klaxons joined to sirens, bells, air-raid hooters, flashing lights outside the Security Area as well as within, had proved irresistible to General Carter.

The initial burst of sound died away, but Alert signal lights went on flashing. The dead silence was more frightening than the noise.

Cramden gripped the edge of his desk and stood up.

"Central Control," he said. "They've got Flint."

He took a stride toward the office door.

"Hand me that loud-hailer, Avery," he ordered. "I got him into this, now I've got to get him out."

Avery sat still, slumped and hopeless.

"You can't, sir," he said. "Remember? You're not allowed into maximum security."

The vigor and pride of command that had upheld Cramden, a burly, vital figure with the energy and drive of a man half his years, ebbed like a wind-blown tide. He wavered back and sat down in his swivel chair, an old man, alone and defeated.

"The odds against him . . ." he said to Avery. "Don't you realize there's no chance? Every device we perfect to trap and destroy an enemy is ranged against our last ally."

Avery could give no better answer than a sigh and an unhappy nod.

Flint's eyes were bright with excitement. Extra reservoirs of adrenalin turned on in his system, a superb fighting machine automatically drawing on its power sources. He swiveled his head from left to right.

The three men moving in from the right were a shade nearer.

Flint moved his arms in a parenthetical arc and cried a karate combat challenge from deep in his throat, a savage growl to match the klaxons themselves.

The primitive cry made the attackers pause just the extra millisecond Flint needed to grasp the first guard at the right by an upper arm and hurl him over his shoulder with a judo throw that sent him smashing into the first attacker on the left.

Flint let momentum carry him all the way around to chop another oncoming guard on the right and shove him low to trip his cohort.

There was a gap now, large enough for a swift rabbit, between Flint and the main stairway.

Flint headed forward and, with a kick that combined karate with the less sportsmanlike aspects of Parisian street-fighting, enlarged the hole wide enough for safe passage.

"He puts on a great performance," Carter admitted to Major Cooper, touching a switch on his light-control panel and picking out Flint with an extra strong spot.

Two more guards followed Carter's cue and blocked the stairway. Flint, after a feint toward them, turned abruptly and made his way to an upward ladder.

Carter's lights picked him up again, but he was scaling the first section before one of the recovered guards of his first assault could reach him. It was easy now for Flint to kick away the hands groping at his feet.

The guard flopped to the tiled floor clutching a broken wrist. Flint climbed higher toward possible safety beyond the moving conveyor belt that led to the disintegrator.

Carter took a microphone from the control panel and barked directions to his forces below. His hands still worked the lighting panel, glaring white paths crisscrossing the walls and floor. Flint dodged between them at various levels, moving from one ladder section to another.

"A-squad move by elevator to upper tiers!" Carter called. "B-squad and C hold lower levels! We've got him on flypaper, boys!"

One of the boys, trying to slug Flint on a catwalk almost parallel with Carter's observation post, heard the General's compliment at the same second that he felt Flint's stone-hard palm edge meet his windpipe. He clutched in reflex at the metal railing, collapsed and fell to the floor below.

A buddy ran to help him, but Carter barked indignation.

"Medics can clean up later. Keep your eye on the ball, men. And Flint's the ball."

Flint managed another ladder climb. He was just above Carter now, but the lights continued to catch his every move. There were two more flights to the conveyor belt and, beyond it, one more tier before the roof section where Flint remembered an exit that might, with all the luck in the world, lead to freedom.

Doors opened at both ends of Flint's narrow ledge. New guards burst out to block retreat.

No opening to his right, no opening to his left, no ladder section within reach.

There was no place to go but up—and the next tier ledge was two feet beyond leaping.

Carter, Austin and Cooper, now looking upward, exchanged satisfied smirks.

Flint crouched and let his assailants come to him. He felled the first with a chop to the temple, the second with a kick.

Hands clutched at him from the other side.

"I thought you'd never get here in time," Flint said, grasping, chopping and piling the third guard on top of the first two.

The fourth attacker fixed two hands in a strangulation grip about Flint's throat. Flint's knee rose high, broke the grip and paralyzed both deltoid muscles.

The first attacker was beginning to move again as Flint placed the fourth body on top of the pile.

"Sorry," Flint said, "but I wasn't planning to stay."

He stepped to the top of the four piled guards, flexed his legs quickly and took a straight-up jump to catch the edge of the tier above. The extra height of the bodies had given him just the footage he needed.

He found the next-to-last ladder without interference. He was above the disintegrator conveyor belt, but now two more sets of guards had joined the battle.

Carter worked his panel frantically. His lights caught only the periphery of the action, but he could see Flint go down under the heavy body of one of his men.

"Stacey's pinned him, Chief!" Cooper yipped.

Had Albert Einstein never lived, the Relativity of Time would still be apparent to anyone experiencing or even witnessing a moment of mortal crisis. The silent struggle of locked bodies on the catwalk could not have lasted beyond some fifty seconds, but to Carter and Cooper and Austin watching from the post below it was an epic battle of timeless duration.

"He's pinned Flint by his jacket!" Austin said.

"He's loose again, dammit!" Carter cursed.

A guard toppled over the edge, pushed against the wall in flight, just missing the conveyor belt to catch himself miraculously on the tier below.

One other guard, catching a jab above his heart from Flint's extended right hand, slumped to oblivion on the ledge. But the odds were still two-to-one and Flint's rasping breath could be heard clearly among the sounds of thumps and scrapings.

"They're both on top of Flint, Chief!" Cooper exulted.

Carter shone what lights he could turn upward into the still-shadowed scene, torn clothing, skin beaded with slippery sweat.

A single dislodged tooth fell in a star-bright arc

through the lights to twinkle incongruously on the tiles and roll between two computers.

There was a sudden groan of triumph and a body fell, reaching hopelessly for the ledge rail, turning in midair before it landed on the conveyor belt. The conveyor belt kept moving on its monotonous way to the disintegrator.

All three heads in the observation booth craned after it. Carter turning his whole battery of lights to flood it.

"Whose?" three voices said together

Carter leaned out farther.

"The jacket!" he crowed. "Flint's ribbons and insignia!"

The huddled lump on the belt passed out of the light and on downward, on toward the macerating steel teeth, on toward the total destruction of sun-hot heat.

"Whew!" Austin puffed.

"We've done it," Carter said, businesslike. "Let's step down and pay our respects. A good man while he lasted. Pity he was on the wrong side."

He flipped his panel switch, turned off the extra flood lights.

"Men!" he spoke into the mike. "Well done. Assemble at 23:35 for debriefing and commendations. Alert medics for any necessary clean-up."

The elevator deposited Carter and his henchmen at the base of the disintegrator assembly, a narrow, reverse funnel chute.

Carter checked his watch.

"Any second now," he said. "Normal operation is two minutes, thirty-three seconds from belt through destruct cogs to furnace to disposal."

At this end, the disintegrator was quite soundless.

There was only a sudden change in the light as a cloud of dust motes began to fall from the chute, picking up rainbow hues in their first thin fall, then, as the flow thickened, appearing only as a dry blast of ashes.

Carter held out an arm and collected a handful.

"Ought to have something to put it in," he said.

"Austin, requisition an urn or something from Burials, G-4," Cooper ordered and Austin scurried to obey.

He was back in five minutes, not only with a tasteful crematory urn (officers' issue in muted gunmetal), but a whiskbroom and a dustpan.

"Good thinking, Aus!" General Carter commended him.

Austin swept and Cooper poured while Carter held the urn. In deference to Flint's former services to the nation, all three men removed their headgear during the operation.

"I'll deliver it to Cramden myself," Carter said, capping the urn with a plastic stopper and leaving Maximum Security for the Executive Offices.

He beat a bright and cheery rat-tat-tat-tat on the frosted glass behind which lights still burned in Cramden's court of shorn authority.

"Come in," Avery called listlessly.

Carter entered, holding the urn before him like a small but charming floral offering to Miss Teenage America.

"Yes, David?" Cramden said from his desk chair.

"Your friend Flint," Carter said, placing the urn on Cramden's Florentine blotter set.

"Flint? What. . . . ?"

"I'm sorry," Carter explained. "The nuclear disintegrator—he sort of fell in."

"Why did you have to kill him?" Cramden asked, sad beyond anger.

"*Mr.* Cramden, I'm surprised at you!" General Carter said. "Flint broke into a Top Security complex. There was no choice."

"He did it because I . . ." Cramden's voice broke as he looked down at the urn.

"I'm sorry," Carter said. "But you know the rules as well as I do, sir."

He executed a smart about-face and left the office.

Avery knew better than to try to phrase either comment or condolence.

He sat silently as Cramden turned the urn in his hands.

"Flint," he said, brokenly. "We had our differences, but this . . ."

5

Outside the security-espionage-nuclear boundaries of Z.O.W.I.E. a slim hand reached inside the wiry bowels of a telephone junction box. The narrow beam of a pen flashlight illuminated its complicated maneuvers as it scraped and spliced a connection in the very center of the labyrinth of crisscrossed, varicolored wires.

In Cramden's office, the ex-Security Chief still sat at his desk. He had uncorked the plastic top of the urn and was gazing at the dusty contents.

"Obstinate," Cramden said, half to Avery, half to his own choking memories. "Obstinate, pig-headed, reckless, a loner—but the greatest."

Avery stood by his side. In an unconscious gesture he started to tip the ash from his filter-tip into the urn on the desk.

"What are you doing?" Cramden bellowed.

Avery drew his hand back and found the ashtray.

"Sorry, sir," he said.

The hands in the telephone maze made a final connection and withdrew. The red phone on Cramden's desk came to life with an insistent buzz.

Perhaps the President had relented!

Cramden snatched the phone from its cradle.

"Yes, sir! . . . Who is this? . . . Flint!!!"

Avery lit a fresh cigarette from his glowing butt.

"What's that, Flint? . . . Don't trust anyone? Right. . . . Yes, yes, I've got that, but, Flint, I've got to see you. . . . What?" Cramden's mouth gaped in incredulity. "Where did you say? . . . Moscow? . . . Why

Moscow? . . . Flint? Flint?" He was speaking into a dead phone.

"He hung up," he said to Avery. "But he's alive. And he's going to Moscow."

"If he's alive," Avery said, pointing to the urn, "who's in there?"

"Who cares?" Cramden smiled, the years slipping away again. "I've got to get to the President."

He spun a forefinger in the dial of the red phone, his direct connection with the White House. An inhuman message met his eager ear.

"This is a recording. You have reached a disconnected number. Please make sure you have the right number before you dial again. Thank you."

Cramden hung up with a jarring rattle.

"I'll see him personally first thing in the morning," he said. He noticed that Avery's cigarette ash was a full inch long.

"Be my guest," he said, shoving the open urn toward his assistant.

A bored but conscientious sentry paced back and forth before the main entrance to Z.O.W.I.E. The alarums and excursions of the Top Security area did not effect his job. Spies and saboteurs were not expected to enter or to leave a government facility by the front door, but there remained the ceremonial duty of patrolling this portal in a proper military manner.

Forty paces forward, halt and about-face, then forty paces to the rear. Halt again before a vibrant recruiting poster. This poster featured a hawk-faced soldier in a mussed-uniform pose implying recent combat, pointing an accusing finger at any Army-age civilian with a conscience.

"Ease off, Mac," the sentry told the poster. "They already got me."

He about-faced and marched away.

The finger-pointing figure detached itself from the poster board. Derek Flint, silent as a Sioux on the warpath, slipped away from the last yards of Z.O.W.I.E. ground.

By the time the sentry turned again, Flint was out of sight, down the street and around a corner. He walked with surface casualness, scanning parked cars. A '66 Mustang looked promising. Flint tried the door, slid in and, with the aid of miniature tools from his lighter, started the ignition in as little time as it might have taken the legal owner to insert his keys.

He gunned the car into the dawn-lightening, deserted street. He sped to a nearby Virginia airstrip.

His Lear was fueled and ready, co-pilot, mechanic and personal handyman standing by.

Flint said, "Take this back to Commonwealth, near the Z.O.W.I.E. gate, and leave it parked, Stupors." And then, having turned the borrowed car over to his handyman, he climbed into the jet and flew away.

In painful contrast to Flint's easy getaway, Cramden, only a few hours later the same morning, was meeting total frustration in his vital effort to see the President. An initial routine call had brought him only the cold tones of a secretary stating that President Muffly's morning was fully scheduled for imporant conferences. Cramden's pleas that his mission concerned matters of top priority were of no avail.

"Well, then, Avery," Cramden said, "I'll fight fire with fire. I haven't been Chief of Security for fifteen years without learning a trick or two."

In the jostle of press photographers wedging toward the President's office, one chunky camera wizard held his Graflex high before his face. At the last door a Secret Service man lowered it forcibly.

"Sorry, sir," he said to Cramden. "Orders are orders."

The group of Boy Scouts entering the Presidential offices an hour later received special solicitude from the middle-aged Scoutmaster who bent over them as he herded them forward. A presidental secretary raised the Scoutmaster out of his face-concealing crouch, shook his head pityingly and showed Lloyd Cramden back out the door.

A delegation of Arab oil royalty twittered in high, liquid tones, moving to their important audience with the Chief Executive of the nation whose corporations paid the royalties which made their eminence possible. But the beard of the next-to-last sheik was grasped rudely by a presidential aide.

"Sorry," he said, "Mr. Cramden."

Balked again, Cramden stomped down the hall, shucked his handsome Arab robe and tossed it into a janitor's closet. Adjusting his tie, he tried the presidential office once again playing himself.

The secretary began the automatic shake of his head, but this time the old security wizard persisted.

"It's about Flint," he emphasized, whispering the last word and glancing warily at the chairs filled with patiently waiting petitioners. "It concerns—and I don't exaggerate, Jackson—President Muffly's own security."

"I can't promise anything," the secretary said. But then, in a whisper infected by Cramden's own solemnity, he relayed the message to the President.

"He'll see you!" he told Cramden in a surprised voice. "Go right in."

"Thank you, Jackson." Cramden stalked triumphantly forward, envy of the still-unadmitted postulants with fruitcake recipes, municipal scrolls, homemade bombs and perpetual-motion schemes.

"Sit down, Lloyd," the President said. "I didn't mean to seem inaccessible, but I assumed your call was about the—uh—hotel matter and I didn't think we'd help anything by hashing it before the official hearing."

"Thank you, sir." Cramden took a chair.

"Now, what's on your mind? And what's happening about our impetuous friend, Mr. Flint?" the President asked. His quick look at his desk clock was not lost on Cramden, who launched into a succinct description of the problem of the missing three minutes.

"Remarkable!" the President said when Cramden paused for breath. *And a damned good thing I did let him in,* he thought silently. "Why didn't you tell me this before?"

"I was afraid, sir," Cramden said, "that you might have thought I'd cracked up. Who could explain a missing three minutes?"

The President drummed a retracted ballpoint pen on his blotter.

"So you felt that Flint might be able to unravel the problem, eh?"

"He seemed my last hope," Cramden admitted.

"And after he broke into Security last night, he told you that we were infiltrated with traitors?" A trace of well-bred disbelief concealed Trent-Muffly's extreme curiosity. He played the bit very well indeed.

"Yes, sir," Cramden said.

"Did he mention any names?" The pseudo-President held his pen quite still, waiting on the answer.

"No, sir," Cramden responded, and the ballpoint resumed its tattoo. "But I believe him. That's why I thought you should know, sir."

"Quite right," Trent said. "I want to thank you, Lloyd. And I want to confess that I misjudged Flint. I'd like to apologize in person. Where is he now?"

"Moscow," Cramden reported.

"What's he doing in Moscow?" the President snarled, momentarily losing his beautiful polish.

"How do I know?" Cramden shrugged. He stretched his arms wide in a gesture of helplessness.

On the great stage of the Moscow Art Theater, Derek Flint stretched his arms wide and high in a gesture of command and control and lifted Natasha Ivanova, premiere ballerina, tenderly aloft to the pulsating music of *Le Spectre de la rose.*

"Derek, darling," the svelte Russian husked in his ear, surprised and gratified to find him replacing her regular partner. "When did you arrive in Moskva?"

"Just hours ago, *cara mia,*" Derek whispered back. "For the beauty of this ballet and the beauty of some moments with you later."

The music swelled and dipped, and Flint released Natasha into the gracefully milling corps de ballet. Strong Russian applause greeted the turns and leaps of his *pas seul.*

Then Natasha had her triumphant solo, then they were linked again in a lift.

As he lowered her, she whispered again into his ear. "The usual place, Derek, my beloved shish kebab?"

"Da."

Flint closed his participation in the number with a leap offstage that broke all existing ballet records. In the wings he thanked the premier danseur whose place he had temporarily taken, and dodged into a dressing room. There he changed to civilian clothes and proceeded to the apartment Natasha kept a stone's throw from the Kremlin.

He was elegant in Savile Row tailoring with a vodka martini at the ready when she turned her key in the door.

She gulped the proffered drink happily.

"Turn me on, man," she begged. "You brought me new records? The Stones That Roll, Mammis and Poppis, Spoons d'amour?"

Flint switched on the portable record player, already stacked with the fresh disc goodies from America.

"Grass in my yard, it can't be weed."

"Sweet Mary Jane, gimme what I need!"

Youthful voices skreeked harshly against a background of electric guitars and an off-key harmonica. Natasha held out her arms and, with Flint responding, frugged wildly through six 45's back and forth through the arched doorway that connected the smart living room with the opulent bedroom—a swan-shaped bed, fur rugs and candelabra—that lay beyond.

"Your American music!" Natasha sighed, falling beside Flint onto an ornate love seat as the last record whirled to its close. "It is so decadent, and yet so exciting. Come, darling, let us now enjoy the champagne."

Flint picked a bottle from its icy nest in a silver bucket.

"A very good year," he said.

"But, of course, darling," Natasha chided. "I been saving it for your regular visit."

Flint poured and touched his glass to the ballerina's.

"And this surprise visit?" he asked.

"A completely delightful event," Natasha said, but Flint sensed a wariness in her sincerity.

They drank with arms interlocked. Flint refilled the glasses.

"You still haven't told me, darling," Natasha said, "why you are here."

Flint lowered his head and kissed her.

"Beyond that," she said a little later.

"My visit concerns two lady cosmonauts," Flint said.

"What would I know about cosmonauts?" Natasha pouted. "And what makes you so certain these are women?"

Flint smiled as her interest and its definition contradicted her pose of innocent ignorance.

"I have a very good reason for my belief," he said. "I read the cardiographs of the cosmonauts in question. The male heart beats seventy-two times a minute. The female, eighty times. *Vive la différence!*"

Natasha spoiled her smooth ivory brow with a frown.

"And these you have read were eighty?" she said.

"Precisely."

She took another sip of her champagne, seeking time to make a decision.

"Very well, darling," she said. "You are right. Two of our Soviet lady cosmonauts are missing. Well?"

"I need your help, Natasha." Flint spoke seriously, putting his champagne glass down on the boule taboret by the love seat. "It's a matter of some importance. Perhaps for you, and Russia, as well as for me."

"There is not ways of deceiving you, Derek," Natasha said, matching his grave mood. "I will tell you all I know."

She reached to the taboret and picked up a cigarette case, taking out two long Russian cigarettes.

"A long story," she said, holding them to Flint. "Fire me up, darling."

Flint took the cigarettes politely, but his smile was now the narrow curve of a hunting shark. He took out his lighter and flicked it to flame, but, before the flame reached the two cigarettes at his lips, he exhaled suddenly and blew it out.

Natasha opened her mouth as if to cry out, but a stern frown from Flint held her silent.

He removed the cigarettes from his own mouth and passed one slowly under his nose.

"Don't move," he said, reaching out an arm and pressing Natasha back against the love seat as she made a motion to rise. "Don't move and don't make a sound."

He sniffed at the cigarette again and then extruded the ringed extension from his fountain pen. As he had done before, he dropped one contact lens into the ring and through it made a minute examination of the cigarettes.

"Virtually the same ingredients," he said. "But I can't understand . . ."

He looked through the lens again and his face brightened.

"Of course," he said. "The paper!"

He stripped off a small amount of paper from the end of the cigarette and gave it the same examination.

"Fibers from the *Agave americana,*" he recited. "A century plant of unusual properties and indigenous to the Virgin Islands."

The shark grin widened. He replaced his fountain pen and, as he did so, noticed on Natasha's vanity table a compact plastic portable hair dryer.

"The missing cosmonauts," he chuckled. "The Virgin Islands."

He picked up the hair dryer and displayed it to Natasha.

"And this last piece to fit into the puzzle," he said. "Fabulous Face is in the Virgin Islands. There is no coincidence. It's all part of the plan."

"Yes," Natasha said with still-friendly defiance. "I can tell you now because you are too late. But do not worry, Derek. It is for the best. For you and for America as well as for me."

Derek Flint was clever, but she and her colleagues—Lisa, Elizabeth, Helena, Simone—had won. Which did not mean that Derek Flint was any the less desirable.

"And now that I have told you," she said, turning to face Flint, "you must make me so happy."

She put her supple arms to his shoulders to draw him to her and then, with a gasp, let them fall.

Framed in the doorway beyond were three men, so thoroughly average in physique and tailoring that they had to be members of the Soviet secret police.

"What is the meaning of this!" she cried and dashed into a furious torrent of Russian, of which Flint caught portions roughly translatable into "Who are you? I have influential friends at the Bureau of Motor Vehicles. If you don't get out this minute you'll regret it!" and "Oh, hell!"

"Nichevo," Natasha said.

"I apologize, Comrade Natasha," the man in the center said, "but our orders come from the Premier himself. He wishes very much to see Mr. Flint."

Flint reached behind the love seat for his jacket, which had been discarded in the exercise of frugging and polite dalliance. The secret police watched him carefully.

"At four-thirty in the morning?" Flint asked, putting his arms into the sleeves.

"He couldn't sleep," the police spokesman explained. "Your performance was so magnificent. He wishes to confer upon you the Nijinsky Medal."

Flint smoothed his lapels and turned to pick up his topcoat.

"Ivan," ordered the head policeman, "help Mr. Flint with his coat."

Really! This was too ancient a gambit to try on a man of Flint's experience.

He let the plainclothesman hold the coat up for him and then rounded with an elbow under the chin that sent the man reeling backward, stunned, as the handcuffs he had been hiding clanked to the marble floor.

Using Ivan as a footstool, Flint vaulted across the intervening bed to the windowsill and stood poised for the merest fraction in time before he soared outward and up.

The third member of the secret police had a handgun at the ready and was taking aim out the window, but the leader pushed his arm down.

"No, Boris," he said reverentially. "Not while he's doing such a beautiful arabesque."

He stayed at the open window long enough to admire Flint's flight and landing on a cornice, then turned back to the room.

"The exterior guards, Boris," he ordered. "And now, beloved Comrade Natasha, let us talk about Mr. Flint."

Mr. Flint had all the roofs of Moscow for his ballet stage.

He had found one essential fact, the prime reason for his journey, and he might have headed at once for safety and home. But there were other things he needed to know, not least among them the possible official involvement of the U.S.S.R. in the slowly unraveling plot.

Therefore his strategy had to be partial rather than total evasion. While the Russian cats thought they were playing with a Yankee mouse, the mouse must play with them and force them to reveal their hand.

A trapdoor on the roof of Natasha's apartment house hinged open. Two trenchcoated men vaulted to the roof. The first one caught a glimpse of Flint crouching only yards away and, with the Kremlin counterpart to a Tally-ho, lunged toward him.

Flint let the man approach within arm's length,

sliced the air with a swift hand chop and was away before the other trenchcoat could catch up. Flint ran along the narrow ledge and took temporary refuge at the base of an onion-shaped minaret surrounded by half a dozen spikey smaller spires. The second trenchcoat caught up and Flint, with a fencer's feint, drew him to the base of the onion, caught him by his coat collar and, clambering to the top of the center minaret, let the secret police agent fall to a smaller onion top.

New reinforcements for the agents were appearing on the roof opposite Natasha's, and this gave Flint a clear path back to reconnoiter the apartment. He ducked among other spires, swung across a roofing gap and found a sheltering icon shape in chiseled granite behind which he could hide and see a section of Natasha's bedroom.

She was sitting huddled on a flimsy feminine chair, the police agent standing in front of her.

"I saw you dance the Swan in Odessa last year," he said in honeyed admiration. "You were wonderful!" He slapped one meaty hand hard across Natasha's face. "Wonderful!" He repeated the slap. Natasha reeled, but held her bleeding lips shut tight.

Another secret police officer, this one in the uniform of a colonel-general, came through the apartment door.

"You waste time, Oleg," he snapped. "We take her to the Premier himself. He is waiting in the war room."

"Da!" Oleg saluted smartly.

Flint ran through a map of Moscow in his head. From here to the Kremlin, then down Communist Street . . .

He retraced his steps, eluding the new trenchcoats on the rooftops until he was two buildings away. The ruse almost worked, but one dawdling agent caught Flint's movement, shouted and pointed him out to a squad of men, some in uniforms and some in trenchcoats, who were piling out of a car in the square below.

Flint ran straight now, speed a better ally than concealment. If he could reach the Nevsky Prospect . . .

He ran a respectable decathlon pace, success assured.

And then, catching himself in his stride before he fell six stories to the cobbled street, he faced the unleapable gap of a broad avenue.

There was no chance of doubling back. The new squad of hunters were already on the same roof.

Flint fumbled with one hand for his lighter as the first trenchcoat pounded toward him. With his free hand he waved and, as the man raised his hands to counter a punch, sent a foot into his chin. His assailant fell sidewise, clutching a pinnacle for support. Flint extended the same free hand in a gentle finger-prod and the agent lost balance, floated free, turning somersaults in the air before he bounced to a landing on the top of the military truck beneath.

The next trenchcoat was only yards away.

Flint pressed a stud in the lighter, releasing a small grappling hook harnessed to a reel of thinnest high-tension wire. Like a surfcaster in top form, Flint let his arm swing forward.

The grappling hook, so small as to be hardly visible in the night's grayness, arced across the street, touched the top cornice of the opposite building . . . and held.

Hands were at Flint's jacket as he brought up his other hand to strengthen his hold on the lighter. He launched himself over the chasm.

The grapple held and the wire held. A human yo-yo, Flint flew above the trees that lined the street, broke his impact against the building with one arm, and clambered over its stone ornamentations, safe for the moment at least.

He crossed the new roof only to find another avenue ahead. No pursuers in sight yet. Taking advantage of more time, Flint threw the grapple again, but made no attempt to swing with it. He checked its grip, then anchored the lighter end deep in a V-cut between two leaning stones.

There was a sound of pounding pursuit. Flint saw three men emerging from a trapdoor on the roof. He bent down to where a thin flagpole proudly supported the Red Star emblem above the front of the building.

One sharp karate blow severed the pole, which he caught and stripped of its ensign.

Flint held the length of pole delicately in hands stretched before him and stepped to the improvised tight-wire. He was a good two-thirds across the gap before the rest of his pursuit arrived at his starting point.

One huge NCO put forward a tentative foot and slipped shaken back into the arms of his companions.

"*Nyet,* nudnik!" a superior scolded. He tugged a heavy knife from his coat and knelt to saw at the steel wire. The tempered tungsten alloy resisted his first efforts and Flint dropped his pole as he reached the next building. Stooping, he caught the grapple end of the wire, let it out an arm's length for slack and gave a quick tug. The lighter was freed from its rock vise and the sudden disappearance of the wire he was trying to cut pitched the sawing officer face first over the roof and onto a terrace below.

He must have held reasonably high rank, Flint thought, watching from behind a chimney pot, for the whole squad halted pursuit efforts to lower themselves to his assistance.

The rest of Flint's journey, uninterrupted by any wide chasms and well shielded from view, was uneventful. Breathing at a normal rate now, he located an air-well hatch in a monumental building of squat, blocky architecture. He sank unnoticed down its narrow shaft. By bracing himself against the sides, he could move down or up without too much effort. He let himself descend some flights until he found a narrow slit of light. It came from the room he had been seeking.

Shielded by shadow, Flint looked through grille and glass into the long, oval-tabled heart of Soviet defense, the U.S.S.R. War Room. Officers, few below the rank of general or admiral, sat at their places around the huge table. Blinking down at them from one entire wall was an illuminated world map. Twinkling, constantly changing lights revealed the locations of all Russian land, air and sea forces in appropriate red, United States and allied congregations in an unhealthy green, a few uncommitted nations in amber. It all reminded Flint of an old espionage film, half-remembered, even down to the middle-class respectability of the worried Russian Premier who was speaking earnestly into the receiver of a red telephone.

Flint ran a hand down his shirt front and removed two buttons. He plugged one in each ear, fixing the wire that connected them to a rubber disc which he pressed onto the window glass.

"Melvin, listen," he heard the Prime Minister's voice in quite passable American English. "If you haven't got our two lady cosmonauts, who has?"

The general next to the Premier nodded grimly.

Flint smiled.

"Melvin," the Premier said, "I've *got* to find those two girls. Be reasonable. . . . They could be *where?* . . . Melvin bite your tongue. They wouldn't live there three days; they hate rice." The Premier sighed. "Melvin, be reasonable. Give me the names of the girls and I'll give *you* the names of our two top spies in America, and will you be surprised. . . You really haven't got them? Melvin, hold on a minute; my secretary is bringing in an important bulletin."

There was a stir at the end of the long room. Flint craned to see Natasha, limp but defiant still, being brought into the room between Boris and another agent.

The commanding agent left the ballerina in Boris's grip and hurried to whisper in the Premier's ear.

"Melvin," the Premier resumed his conversation, "I'll make a deal with you. All right, you say you haven't got the girls, but just in case you're kidding, we've got Flint. . . . Who? Flint, F as in Flint, L as in Lenin, I as in Ivanovitch, N as in Nyet, T as in Trotsky, I mean Tsar, hell, T."

His right-hand general leaned into the phone as the Premier listened incredulously to the presidential answer.

"Yes, Flint," he repeated. "What? Kill him? But he's your number-one hero . . ."

The general whispered to the admiral on his right. The room buzzed with awed reaction.

Natasha, as the word reached her, broke into uncontrolled sobbing.

"Well, listen, Melvin," the Premier recovered some aplomb. "I was exaggerating. We don't actually have him, but we know where he's going. A little bird told me." He beamed at Natasha. She spat and Boris gave her another clout in the chops.

"Yes," the Premier went on. "The Virgin Islands. . . . Melvin, you know we have no flights there. Only to Cuba."

At his ventilator-shaft window, Flint nodded as he made a mental note.

"Melvin," the Premier asked in a worried voice, "what would Flint want in Cuba? I'll talk to you again, Melvin, and thanks for accepting the call."

He hung up.

"Nichevo!" he said to the assembled military.

Flint waited until he could be sure the crisis conference was actually adjourning. Then, raising himself by pressure of elbows, knees and feet, he began a slow progress back up the shaft.

6

Nudging fleecy white clouds over Finland as it banked into a southwesterly turn, the giant Soviet jet transport looked from the ground like a long silver fish flirting with flecks of cotton wool. The interior, stripped of the luxury reserved for commercial flights, was an airborne bucket-seated bus full of Cuba-bound passengers.

The passenger list could have been assembled from a documentary on Fidel Castro, Sierra Madre to today. Pro or con, Cuban revolutionaries were hung up on the same wardrobe, facial hair and general characteristics. Bearded men of all sizes and shapes, slumped sleeping in their seats, played dominoes, argued about Albania and China, passed rum bottles back and forth, walked up and down the center aisle, scratched themselves, adjusted their ammunition bandoliers (without which any one of them would have felt embarrassingly naked) for greater dozing comfort.

One tall guerrilla type sprawled in sleep over two seats, his scraggly beard rising and falling with his breath, a man plumbing the depths of Morpheus for recovery after hard chores. The wristwatch above one sinewy hand showed a growing glow from its dial as the winding stem moved out two millimeters and turned so that a small prong pecked into its wearer's flesh.

Flint awoke; much refreshed.

He stood up in the aisle, stretched, yawned and, to be socially conforming, ran fingernails about his chest with ardent ecstasy. He had been able to sleep out almost the whole flight and his system, always quick on the rebound, was back to its normal supernormality.

Leaning down among his jostling fellow travelers, Flint reached under his seat and removed the limp and scraggly carcass of a dead chicken.

"Mi almuerzo," he explained to a curious beard as he moved along to the front of the plane. "Lonch." He plucked random patches of feathers from the dead bird as he walked.

A pert Intourist stewardess sat in her place at the entrance to the pilots' cabin.

Flint gave her a courtly bow and shoved the now almost featherless chicken into her hands.

"Arroz con pollo," he gave his dinner order with a flashing smile. The smile, reinforced by her handsful of chicken, stopped the girl short of protest as Flint passed her and opened the door to the cabin. He closed it behind him. The girl followed him with her eyes, but, when there was no sound or signal from the cabin, she devoted herself to examining the chicken.

These visiting satellite military, you could never tell. This one must be a big shot to be accepted in the pilots' quarters. . . .

The jet went into a sharp bank and several beards fell against each other, entangling their bandoliers. The hostess, in a hopeful mixture of Spanish and Russian, suggested that they fasten their seatbelts and refrain from smoking. The passengers scowled, continued lurching up and down the aisle, and an independent few (the pro-Albania factionists) lighted cigars.

Cramden, wishing he had never given up cigars, chewed on a pencil in his office, found it didn't draw well and threw it into the wastebasket.

"What's going on, Avery?" he cried. "I get to the President's office and think I'm going to have a good old-time talk. When I mention that Flint's in Moscow, he can hardly wait to get rid of me. People I've never even heard of are placed in key positions, new faces everywhere. And the date of my hearing postponed indefinitely. . . . If Flint is right and we've been infiltrated, we're in real danger."

Carried away by the intensity of his emotion, he put a fresh pencil in his mouth, lit a match and clamped down on the wood with a full bite before the first gratifying puff. The pencil shattered and Cramden roared.

"Avery! This damned thing is alive. I'm being electrocuted!"

His aide was at his side.

"If you'll stop swearing, sir," Avery said, prying at Cramden's mouth, "I think I can get it out."

"Takc it easy," Cramden pleaded, twisting his jaws in pain.

"I've got it, sir!"

Avery withdrew the pencil end, but stared at it in transfixed horror instead of throwing it to join its predecessors in the wastebasket.

Cramden rose to see what was up.

"A transmitter!" he said. "They've known every move we've made."

"But who are *they,* sir?" Avery asked.

"I don't know." Cramden took the miniaturized snooper and turned it over in his hands. "But I was right. And Flint was, too. How can we trace them?"

"I think I may have a way, sir," Avery said excitedly. "This device should work on the same principle as a walkie-talkie."

"So?" Cramden loved every gadget in the security arsenal, but had always left techniques to the technicians.

"That means the system can be reversed, sir. The sending apparatus can become a receiving set."

Avery whispered, taking the shredded pencil end and placing it on Cramden's blotter. He opened a small penknife and made inroads among the wires.

"Just a moment, sir," he said, squinching his eyes to make reverse connections.

"There, sir. I believe that does it."

The two men's heads bent together over the blotter. From the rejiggered transmitter came confused humming sounds, a faint garble of voices . . .

. . . a faint garble of voices above the humming of the TV monitors in General Carter's office where the monitor screens showed, left to right, the interior of the launch site for the second space-platform load, its exterior, and the loading of the missile not with the scheduled additional space-platform hardware but with nuclear warheads.

"All going well," General Carter said to Major Cooper.

A blink-light signal flashed over the first interior monitor set. Carter could see a worried-looking Air Force first lieutenant pressing his communication button.

Carter took the call on his desk mike, his words now transmitted precisely to Cramden and Avery.

"General Carter, here."

"General Carter, sir? General Carter?"

"Here. What is it, lieutenant?"

"Sir." The lieutenant's voice quavered. "This orders me to load the rocket with nuclear bombs. Not the weather lab we had ready for the space platform. Nuclear bombs, sir?"

"That's right, lieutenant," General Carter confirmed crisply. "Project Damocles."

"Pro . . . project Damocles?" The lieutenant still faltered. "Arming the space platform, sir?"

"That's correct," Carter said. "The code name is Damocles. New orders directly from the White House. This is Top Security. You understand, lieutenant?"

The magic words had their effect. The lieutenant stiffened to military obedience on the monitor screen.

"Yes, sir," he said back, as crisply as Carter himself. He turned and pressed another switch at his own desk. "Proceed with arming immediately. Proceed."

Cramden, listening with Avery two buildings away, gripped the edge of his chair, trembling with disbelief and dismay.

"Arming the space platform," he said. "Do you realize the consequences, Avery?"

"A nuclear threat to the whole world," Avery said as if reciting by rote. "A betrayal of every international agreement since the Test Ban Treaty." He wiped sweat from his forehead with the cuff of his sleeve. "And he said, sir, that the orders came from the White House."

"We know Melvin Muffly better than that, Avery," Cramden said. Behind his eyes raced a panorama of reunions at Princeton, the Chicago Convention, presidential fishing trips and golf games, long talks into the night at Camp David. "General Carter is a traitor. He's got to be stopped."

The old iron man rose from his swivel chair.

"I'm going to see the President," he said.

"Should I remain here, sir?" Avery asked.

"Yes, keep listening. Every word may be valuable. Every minute counts now."

"Every minute counts," Cramden pounded on the desk of the presidential secretary.

"I'm sorry, Mr. Cramden," the secretary said, "but that's what everyone says who wants to see the President. You had a meeting only the other day, sir. I have specific instructions about who may be admitted. . . . Sir! Guards!"

Cramden had lost his sorely tried patience. He shoved the secretary to one side, knocked over a Secret Service man with a Flintian shoulder-shove and burst open the door of the President's office.

Trent-Muffly looked up from his revery with well-bred surprise.

"I'm sorry, sir," the secretary clawed futilely at Cramden's coattails. "He insisted." He motioned to the Secret Service men crowding after him, but the President as quickly waved them back.

"That won't be necessary, Jackson," he said. "I don't believe Mr. Cramden, of all people, intends any harm to me."

"Thank God!" Cramden said.

"I'm glad to see you're still physically fit, Lloyd," the President said drily, catching a glimpse through the door of the one dislodged guard getting up from the floor.

"I'm sorry," Cramden said, still short of breath. "It was of the utmost importance that I see you, sir."

"I'm sure of that," the President said. "All right, Lloyd, what's troubling you?"

It was the true Melvin Muffly man-to-man manner, the manner that got way-back Texas oil barons to sit down to dinner next to way-out college professors, that made cause-conscious youth-group leaders join stand-pat clubladies to form a landslide organization chanting in unison "Muffly for President."

Just to hear it warmed Cramden's badly bruised heart.

"It's very personal, sir," he said, looking toward the secretary.

"You may go, Jackson," the President said.

Cramden waited until the door had chunked fully closed.

"Sir," he said. "I have definite evidence that General Carter is a traitor."

The President, who had picked up a golf club and was swinging idly in perfect imitation of the President, stopped his swing and stared sharply at Cramden.

"That's a serious accusation, Lloyd," he said. "What proof do you have?" His voice was still Muffly, but his eyes had narrowed to a shifty alertness.

"The space platform is going to be armed," Cramden said in one pained breath. "The orders, sir, supposedly came from you."

"Do you believe that, Lloyd?" he asked with quiet dignity.

"Knowing you as I do?" Cramden said. "Of course not."

"Lloyd," the President said in the same sincere note, "the human mind is a very fragile instrument. It can take just so much stress, and then it rebels. Sometimes, Lloyd, it has strange ways of rebelling."

"Sir," Cramden drew himself up indignantly. "I assure you that—"

"How long has it been since you've had a complete checkup?" the President asked gently.

"It *has* been quite a while, sir," Cramden admitted. "Every time I make an appointment at Walter Reed there's some damned crisis and I have to break it. But I—"

Trent raised one finger from his grip on the golf club.

"The restaurant incident," he said. He raised another finger. "The hotel affair." Another. "Your loss of memory." A fourth. "And now these, ah, unusual allegations."

"If you're suggesting, sir, that I have cracked up . . ." Cramden still bridled.

"I am not a psychiatrist, Lloyd," the President said evenly. "But as a veteran, you are entitled to the best. As an old friend, Lloyd, take advantage of our facilities. Think of the friends we've known in St. Elizabeth's. . . . If you'll excuse me now . . ."

Cramden's lips framed another protest, but diplomacy killed it before it could emerge. Whatever was happening had President Muffly, for all his honesty and high ideals, firmly entangled in its web. Cramden could no longer count on old friendship and past achievement to break this enchantment; not, at least, until he had more concrete and undeniable evidence.

"Thank you, sir," he said, leaving the office with his shoulders bowed under too much weight for one aging man.

Trent grinned at his retreat.

"Get me General Carter," he said in a low voice into one of his telephones.

"Sir?" Avery asked optimistically as Cramden came back to the quarantined office.

"Nothing!" Cramden spat.

"But your evidence—"

"Mental fatigue! Hallucinations!" Cramden ranted. " 'I'm not a psychiatrist, Lloyd, but as an old friend . . .' Dammit, maybe I *am* going mad!"

He glared angrily at the pencil transmitter on his desk.

"No sir," Avery assured him. "Remember, I heard

it, too. Something's very wrong. If we could only get to Flint."

"Get to Flint. . . ." Cramden forced his mind from self-pity to action.

He rumpled his cropped hair as if to induce a train of thought and the gimmick-habit worked.

"We can find him!" he crowed. "He was going to meet his girls. That's it, Avery! They're at some beauty resort with a silly name—someplace in the Virgin Islands."

"Virgin Islands?" Avery responded with excitement. "But that's where . . ."

He rummaged through the flip maps on an easel-like stand, Cramden following his thought, helping him. They stopped at a large-scale Top Secret chart of the Caribbean. Cramden's stubby finger found a red-circled clot of square, round and oblong black dots.

"The launch site," Cramden said. He traced downward from the red circle to a promontory which jutted from the coastline. He read the printed legend: " 'Fabulous Face.' That's the beauty spot."

"Amazing coincidence," Avery murmured.

"Coincidence, hell!" Cramden said. "It's all linking up. Avery, you head for the missile site at once."

"Yes, sir." Avery stood at attention. "And you?"

Cramden had a cat's grin surmounting his bear's body.

He went back to his desk and opened the top drawer. From it he removed a small hand mirror and a cordless electric shaver. Wordlessly, he propped the mirror to a utility position and started to shave off the gray-flecked moustache that had been for so long his trade mark, the proud blaze of personality familiar to millions of newsreel and television watchers, adornment of one cover of *Time* magazine, ornament of a thousand newspaper photographs.

Avery watched, a little shaken. It was like watching someone deliberately mutilating the Lincoln Memorial by chiseling off the beard of the Great Emancipator.

"I wasn't always a chairborne commando," Cramden

said above the relentless buzzing of the shaver. "And Flint isn't the only master of disguise. Before you go, stop in at Kann's and get me a size 18 matron's suit. Any kind of blouse will do as long as it doesn't swear at my eyes."

Truly awed, Avery left the office.

President-nonelect Trent-Muffly sat at his immense desk, signing papers, waiting on the arrival of General Carter. Although his squad of secretaries did all the ground work, screening and separating those few documents that required a real presidential signature from the mass that were signed by them in reasonable facsimile, Trent enjoyed checking over the typescripts.

Here, with a stroke of the pen, he welcomed an African president to a week in Washington. Here, with another swift scribble, he made possible a dam which would flood seventy odd farms in the Midwest, but supply new agricultural water for six times that number. Here he consoled a GI widow for her husband's death on combat in a distant police action. Here he slapped down a bumptious representative from New England who wanted his wife's great-grand-uncle's portrait to appear on a postage stamp.

It was exciting work, ever various and always with the buoying headiness of power.

The outer-office secretary's buzzer sounded. Trent pressed an answering beep okaying entrance. General Carter, a splendid figure bearing the insignia of his new rank, entered.

"Be right with you." The President looked up from his papers. "Just have to sign these bills. Conservation, air safety, National Plastic Teething Ring Week."

Carter walked quietly about the office while Trent finished his signature work. The General unconsciously let his hand graze against the various pieces of furniture, each one with some historic or contemporary magic attached to it, used by another Chief Executive at a time of peril and triumph, gift of a grateful allied nation across the ocean, personal choice of a gracious First

Lady who lived on now only as a fading, rather stilted nineteenth-century portrait in the Smithsonian Institution. It was a room to make any man pause and think.

Trent scrawled the last signature and stacked the signed papers into a neat pile on the Outgoing section of his desk.

"That's it, Dave," he said.

General Carter was looking at him quizzically.

"You like being President, don't you?" the General asked.

"Very much," Trent admitted. He picked up a paper from the top of the just-completed pile and held it up. "Do you realize," he said, "the power of this signature? The most important in the world."

Carter nodded.

"Too bad you're going to have such a short term in office," he said.

Trent leaned back and let his swivel tilt to executive comfort.

"Maybe not," he said, his own voice replacing the Muffly imitation. "It's the best performance I've ever given. It deserves a long run."

He smiled up at Carter and Carter smiled back with a venal leer.

"Why not?" Carter said. "But what I came about—Cramden's headed for Fabulous Face."

"See that he's taken care of personally," Trent said.

"Right," Carter said, hesitating a second before adding: "Sir."

"Sit down a minute, Carter." Trent was confidential. He looked again at the stacked papers bearing his presidential signature. "I think maybe we've done enough for the girls. . . . Carter, how would you like to be the *second* most powerful man in the world?"

Carter's jackal grin widened. He nodded his head, drew it closer to the President's.

The pilot and co-pilot of the Russian airliner over the Caribbean, bound and gagged, looked on as Flint checked his bearings one last time, set the automatic pilot, buckled on his chute pack and opened the door to the passenger section.

He walked down the aisle and opened the exit door.

"Ho, mira!" the stewardess exclaimed.

"Adiós, amigos," Flint bade the Cuban congeries farewell. "Just now I have to drop in on some friends."

He stepped out into space above the Virgins.

7

Daylight drenched Fabulous Face.

The Heirloom Hair-room was, as usual, factory-like and fully occupied. Its long parallel rows of dryers resembled so many inverted egg cups on pedestals, each cup capping a feminine head. Functionally designed chairs held the dryer customers, with foot rests and hand rests for pedicures and manicures. Adjacent tables were stacked with the latest beauty-parlor literary fare—magazines emblazoned with bright headlines above proud feminine faces: "HAS JACKIE FOUND HAPPINESS WITH A TEENAGER?" (about Mrs. Kennedy and her son Jon-Jon), and a majority of more bristling titles: "ARE MEN OBSOLETE? asks Starlet Boots Walker"; "WHY NATALIE SAYS 'NEVER AGAIN' "; "THE MEN IN MY LIFE and Other Pigs"; "TARZAN'S MATE TELLS ALL."

Up and down the line of dryers, uniformed Amazon attendants performed their services, scraping cuticles, tinting fingernails, reforming misshapen toes, checking dryer temperatures and, most importantly, checking the punched tapes that curled from the rear aperture slit of every dryer.

The tape girl read off data quickly and made necessary but infrequent notes on a small stenographic pad. However, when she reached the three dryers sheltering the beautiful heads of Flint's girls, Jan, Terry and Denise, she slowed, stopped fully, and compressed her lips (Fabulous Face Ski-Dawn #7) in bewilderment.

The treatment had never before been known to fail, but there was something different about these three girls. Here they were in their second day of maximum exposure, yet the tape symbols read as if they'd never been under an FF dryer before.

She checked again. All three tapes gave approximately the same reading, and all three tapes were uniformally disappointing. She tore them off the dryers and beckoned for another attendant.

"I'd better take these upstairs," she said. "Something's seriously wrong with these gals, Hilda."

Hilda ran an experienced eye over the tapes.

"Not much that I can see," she said, "for new . . . But they aren't new. Something fishy. Maybe the machines are out of whack."

"Just these three?" the tape checker shook her head. "Uh uh. These girls have built-in resistance. We're just not reaching them. That Flint must make quite an impression." She found her own trained mind speculating on quite unusual channels and disciplined herself before she could verbalize traitorous thoughts. "I better take these upstairs. *They'll* know what to do. You mind the store, Hilda."

Hilda, her own curiosity piqued, moved to the front of Jan's chair.

Jan smiled from under the dryer's hood.

"May I manicure those lovely hands?" Hilda asked with professional flattery that, for once, was sincere. "We have a brand-new nail color, dear. Emerald Frappe, just out today. It's the wildest, toughest—"

"Oh, is that another one of those greenish-silvery shades?" Jan questioned pleasantly. "No, thanks. We don't use any of those. You see, Derek only likes shades of red."

"Shades of red!" Hilda's indignation was almost a squeak, a Sarah Lawrence undergraduate discovering that a close friend had kind words for the Spanish Inquisition. "But my dear, how passé. How utterly eighteenth century!"

Her raised voice had carried to the next dryer, from which Terry tilted her golden-haloed head.

"Tell you the truth," Terry confided, "I kind of dig those crazy colors, but since Derek doesn't love them, what's the point?"

"What's the point?" Hilda could not stop sounding shrill. "Wake up, honey! A girl should wear what *she* likes, not what some wall-eyed man thinks *he* likes. What if your Derek happened to like whalebone corsets and hoopskirts?"

Hilda preened herself on an ultimate put-down, but Terry just giggled mischievously.

"But that's just silly," she said. "Derek *hates* corsets."

She looked about her at the audience of heads which had popped from surrounding dryers in response to the noise of her exchange with Hilda.

"But he *likes* red nail polish," she repeated. "Who do you try to get pretty for if not your man?"

If a public-relations representative of the National Association of Manufacturers had suddenly begun addressing typical NAM sentiments to a high-level policy conference in Peking, he could hardly have caused more consternation.

"Your *man?"* Hilda skreeked. "Good Lord, why? That's—medieval!"

Other attendants and dryer clients took up the chant.

"Positively barbaric!"

"I suppose she'd wear a ring in her nose if some man said he liked it!"

"Was it for this Amelia Bloomer suffered?"

"Carrie Chapman Catt . . . !"

Hilda, at last able to lower her voice below a protesting shriek, began explaining to other attendants the peculiar problems of the three Flint girls.

Jan, Terry and Denise themselves were more amused than upset.

Eventually, after some wheedling by the staff, most heads withdrew into dryers and the Heirloom Hairroom once more presented something like its normal appearance.

Hilda exhaled with relief. She had been at Fabulous Face for more than a year now and nothing like this had ever happened before.

"I guess the machines were telling the truth," she said to a sister attendant.

Jan, still partly out of her dryer helmet, peered at her inquiringly.

"You gals may be obsolete," Hilda said, her Amazon armor breeched to near-companionability, "but I'd sure like to get a look at that boyfriend of yours."

She adjusted the three dryers to a notch higher in the indoctrination-intensity scale and wondered whether it would do any good.

"I can't explain it," the tape checker was reporting to Lisa in the penthouse executive office. "These girls have resisted all our programming, Miss Norton. This Mr. Flint of theirs—"

"Is a man, nothing more!" Lisa said sharply, eyes still on the Countdown Clock that counted silent seconds on her desk. "Our Intelligence reports he's headed here. I suggest you place his girls in cold storage until we can get rid of him. They are obviously useless at the moment."

"Cold storage?" The tape-check attendant put a manicured hand to her mouth in surprise. "The Cryobiology Room?"

"Yes." Lisa was firm. "They're fine, stubborn girls, just the kind we'll need some day, but we haven't time to play educational games with them now."

"Save for later programming?" the attendant asked.

"Right," Lisa said, dismissing her and making a notation of the reading on the Countdown Clock.

The telephone on the cabinet by her desk rang. She picked it up.

"Airport Observations? . . . Thank you, dear, I'll see that it's attended to at once."

She snapped on her intercom to the dryer assembly line.

"Hilda!" she called. "I have a little assignment for you. Greetings Division for uninviteds. In about ten minutes."

In nine and a half minutes the sleek Fabulous Face airport limousine was stopping smoothly at the entrance stair to the resort reception salon. The Amazonish chauffeur, chic in a uniform of sky-blue blouse and denim hipsters, opened the door for the new guest.

A bulky figure, obviously hot and uncomfortable in a tweed suit that might have been worn by Margaret Rutherford playing Miss Marple, grunted its way out the door and almost snapped a high heel making a landing from car to curb.

Unconsciously, Lloyd Cramden stroked at the space where his moustache had always been for a reassurance not forthcoming.

"Damn!" he muttered.

"Welcome to Fabulous Face, Mrs. Hiller!" Hilda trilled, stepping up to take his valise. "Your room is ready. Just follow me, please."

"Gronkles!" Cramden said. He had meant to say thank you in the high-pitched ladylike accent he had been practicing to himself all the way down on the plane, but the obvious hazards of the long stairway stretching before him smothered intelligible speech.

Hilda held back her smile.

"Seventy steps to beauty, we call it," she said sunnily leading the way, swinging the valise easily at her side.

Cramden hugged the wall, tried to walk on tippy-toes rather than trust any portion of his two hundred fifty plus pounds to the slender mercy of his teetering heels. A knot of Fabulous Face clients observed his and Hilda's descent with mingled wonder and terror.

"Now that's what I call ambition!" one girl said, running her eyes over Cramden's lumpy figure.

He paused midway down the stairs to tug pettishly at his girdle, which had taken advantage of the new activity to ride up and become a torturing rubberized noose well above the area where it was supposed to work its slenderizing magic.

"I think it's sweet." A more romantic young woman observed Cramden's sweaty progress. "I can see her scrubbing floors, year after year, saving quarters, dollars at a time for the whole treatment down here."

"I think she waited about five years and a hundred pounds too long," a friend said dubiously.

"But don't you see," the romantic insisted earnestly, "*anything* they do for her is going to be an improvement."

"But those calves!" the other girl moaned.

Cramden's imperfectly shaven legs bulged from their nylons like prize-winning country sausages at a Pennsylvania Dutch fair.

"They do present a problem," the romantic admitted. "But massage, the steam room, elastic stockings—"

"Nothing less than surgery," the other girl said firmly. "Actually, amputation."

Cramden reached the reception patio at the foot of the stairs with a wheeze of victory.

"This way, dear," Hilda encouraged him, turning off down a long corridor.

Cramden followed a little more confidently. An air-conditioned room, he thought. Kick off these damned shoes and lie down for ten minutes or so. Then on with the chase.

Hilda opened a door and stood beaming hospitality beside it.

The weary traveler quickened his pace to enter.

"Hey!" he cried. He saw no luxury bed, no picture window, no pastel tints. He saw only two crude prison-style cots in double-decker style, an ancient washbowl and a gray, windowless wall. "Hey!"

But Hilda had tossed his valise in after him and slammed the door. He heard the chunking click of a heavy lock snapping into place.

Cramden spun around. He pounded on the door.

"No use," said a familiar voice from the shadow.

He turned back and saw an unshaven face staring from the upper bunk.

"Mr. President!" Cramden quavered in shock and surprise. "What are you doing here?"

The President was trying to bring his eyes into focus in the room's dim light.

"Lloyd?" he said tentatively, and Cramden's whole burden of jumbled speculations fell into place.

"I was right," he said. "The golf course, the missing minutes—"

"Lloyd, please," the President said miserably. "Tell me. Why am I here? What's going on?"

Despite his outlandish costume, Cramden squared his shoulders and won back some of his old dignity. Hopeless as the present situation seemed, he was once again the Security Chief reporting to his Chief Executive.

"You'd better lie back down, Mr. President," he said. "There's quite a bit to tell."

And he started to unfold the events of the past days . . .

. . . as Flint, chute jettisoned in the sea, swam with long, powerful strokes toward the shore . . .

. . . as Denise, Jan and Terry in the dryer room continued to chafe at the most intensive treatments Fabulous Face could, overtly, offer them.

By now they were the only three guests left in the Heirloom Hair-room. They had read all available editions of *Vogue* and *Harper's Bazaar*, current and past, and made a dent in the stacks of lesser beauty and film magazines. What had loomed brightly as a great fun vacation was turning into a dismal grind.

"There goes the last of them." Denise watched a plump Scarsdale matron leave her dryer and make for the pool. "And here we sit. This is getting to be a real bore, kids."

"It was the same thing yesterday," Jan complained. "Some Caribbean holiday, hooked to a hair dryer."

"I haven't even gotten a tan yet." Terry added her gripe. "Seems to me we're under these things longer than anybody else in the joint."

A group of attendants came in on Terry's plaint—Hilda, the tape-checker who had reported to Lisa, and four husky teammates.

"We don't prescribe the treatments, dear," the checker answered Terry's overheard dissatisfaction. "That's all individual diagnosis, you know. Put together from your fact file."

"Well, somebody must think our hair is in pretty tough shape," Jan said. "Personally, and if you ask me, cooking it for hours on end like this isn't going to help much."

"I can feel mine turning to alfalfa right now," Jan said. "It'll take about three oil shampoos to bring it back."

The attendants made little soothing noises, bustling about and disconnecting the machines.

"There now," Hilda said, taking the dryer cone from Terry's head. "Isn't that better?"

The other Amazons had freed Jan and Denise.

"Just one more session," Hilda said, "and we're all through for the day."

"How about a swim, first?" Terry asked, but firm, gentle hands were coaxing her along with Denise and Jan out of the room and through a passage to the rear.

"Well, whatever's coming up, I hope it'll at least be cool," Denise sighed.

The tape-checker, leading, turned back with a freckled, boyish grin.

"You can count on that, dearie," she said. "This way."

The girls and their accompanying squad went down a short flight of stairs. The tape-checker opened the door on a long, narrow underground room lined with sealed cubicles of uniform size, six by three by two, stacked together in rows.

"What do you get down here?" cracked fun-loving Terry. "Embalming?"

The Amazons chuckled.

"Straight ahead, dear," Hilda said.

But Jan had stopped to read the neatly incised lettering on the marble slab above the banks of cubicles.

"Cryobiology!" she said. "Cryobiology!" pointing out the sign to Denise and Terry. "You know what that is? That's the latest mad-doctor fad—quick-freezing people to bring them back to life later. Maybe!"

Hilda pinioned Jan's arms behind her.

The other attendants subdued the other two girls. Flint had let the trio share some of his judo training, but mostly as a lark. They lacked the total skills of their employer and, caught now by surprise and in the narrow passageway, outnumbered, they didn't stand a chance.

The soundproof doors of the Cryobiology Lab eased open. A bevy of even huskier technicians took the girls, one by one, into the deep-freezing section.

"You'll be all right, honey," Hilda assured Jan as she passed her through. "They just want you out of the way for a little while."

"Not to worry," Denise's captor soothed.

"They'll let you out as soon as they get rid of your Mr. Flint," another Amazon told Terry, shoving her along toward the chill atmosphere beyond the door.

The interior technicians slammed the door to. The attendants smoothed the uniforms from the muss of the brief struggle.

"I sort of hated to do that," the tape-checker said. "They're such nice kids. What a pity they're so hard to convince."

"It's that Flint of theirs," Hilda said thoughtfully. "He must be a hypnotist or something."

The squad of Amazons fell into unnatural silence, walking slowly back up along the corridor. Exposure to Terry, Denise and Jan had been short, but long enough to start thoughts stirring in their heads unsanctioned by the official philosophy of Fabulous Face.

"A hypnotic trance?" one girl thought aloud. "No. The dryer conditioning would break it in no time, wouldn't it?"

"Something more than hypnotism," one of her buddies said. "It seemed like this Flint was all they could talk about, no matter what."

"Does it ever make you wonder?" the tape-checker considered. "I mean, when you see how girls like that feel, if maybe men do have something—"

"I'm wondering right now," Hilda admitted.

"I'd give a week's pay for a look at that Mr. Flint!" the tape-checker burst out. "Wherever he is."

A look at Mr. Flint would have found him treading water near the outer reaches of the Fabulous Face beach.

He had made good time, swimming at an even pace that did not leave him winded for the work ahead. Now he half-floated, stymied by a barbed-wire fence looming outward from the jagged rock outcroppings of the breakwater facing him.

He let the tide carry him some yards down. The same barrier.

He swam twenty yards in the other direction. Barbed wire and rock as far as his eyes could reach.

"Situation where a chap needs some friendly natives," Flint verbalized his thought. "I wonder . . ."

Still treading water he opened his mouth and began to emit a series of eerily strange sounds, staccato whistles of varying lengths, shrill yips and barks almost at the limit of human sound.

He stopped his concert and stayed as still as he could, ears strained. A few small sound waves, all but inaudible to any ear untrained by constant practice, brought a smile to Flint's face.

He ducked and surface-dived beneath the warm waves. Checking his direction from the shore, he swam several yards to the right to come face to face with the glistening, round, amiable bulk of a giant dolphin.

Flint squeaked another series of sounds. The dolphin, his curved mouth seeming to break into a smile, answered in similar yips.

Flint waved a hand to the shore and the dolphin shook a fin impatiently.

More squeaks and yips and signals ensued. Finally the dolphin, with the shrug of a Manhattan pedestrian giving up trying to make a foreigner understand the location of Grant's Tomb, signaled "Follow me!" quite distinctly.

The dolphin dived deeper and Flint dived after it. They swam almost shoulder to shoulder, so to speak, Flint a little to the rear, up along the shoreline. The dolphin, seeming to understand Flint's crude breathing needs, let him surface there before another dive. Then another four minutes took them plunging through cooler, fresher water.

When they surfaced this time, it was just inside the ocean-bound course of a riverlet which ran beneath coral bastions to its Caribbean outlet.

"Thanks," Flint said and, remembering his companion's species, translated the courtesy into new yips.

The dolphin yipped back a "Don't mention it," wagged a fin in farewell and was gone.

The river current was weak and placid this near its broad outlet. Flint swam effortlessly upstream for half a mile.

A waterfall, plunging with a diamond glitter over a hundred feet from above, stopped his swim. Oncoming night painted the falling water black through dark blue to the glowing white of bursting spume touched by moonlight.

Flint gave up swimming and waded to the foot of the falls. Its rocky texture presented no difficulties to a man who had scaled K-2 on a dare. Halfway up he took a shortcut through a crevice in the rocks and came out into water deep enough to continue his swimming.

He ran through the detailed geodetic survey map of the area he had imprinted in his head before leaving. Twenty more yards should bring him within the official confines of Fabulous Face.

He sniffed cautiously and slowed his pace. Holding close to the bank, he came around a slight bend in the river and into the faintly sulphur-tinged, vapor-veiled waters that marked The Pool of Youth, Fabulous Face's famed aqueous bounty of health and beauty.

At the pool edge across from him he could make out

the extravagantly shapely shapes of four customers enjoying the treatment. They appeared, from Flint's vantage point, to be following the advice in the Fabulous Face brochure, to wit, that any bathing garment, even a bikini, could only interfere with the full restorative power of the waters.

The brunette at the end was fantastic. She arched her back and slid into the pool and Flint sighed at a deadline which forced him onward. He pulled himself out of the water and slid into the bougainvilleas clustering on the banks. Swiftly and silently he sought a safe area where he could repair his wardrobe.

Sure that he had gone, a girl at the poolside picked up a telephone shielded by the sulphurous vapors.

"Penthouse," she directed. "Yes, please. . . . This is the Pool of Youth attendant, Miss Lisa. The gentleman just passed by." She giggled into the phone. ". . . I don't know about that, ma'am. He wasn't exactly dressed for visiting."

Flint, in the bowered glade he had found, pulled a compact oilskin packet from his trunks, opened it and removed three smaller packages.

He undid the fastening of the first one, shook it as if he were cracking a whip, and revealed a light-weight jacket of orlon and a new synthetic as yet only labeled Y17. As he shook it, molecular memory restored its creaseless tailoring. He hung it over one arm. Then he snapped open the other two small packets and produced a pair of tapered slacks and a clean shirt. He donned the dry clothing, ran a hand through his hair to satisfy himself of its neatness, and prepared to reconnoiter the resort buildings.

Illumination of the grounds at Fabulous Face was romantically dispersed. Flint found it easy to move from his alfresco dressing area to the side of the first building and to work his way along its wall to the nearest window.

Looking through, he saw an evening shift of guests exercising in the gymnasium area. Girls in shorts and halter, girls in slacks, and poorboys, and girls in overalled sweatsuits toiled at rowing machines, pedaled grimly on exercycles, lay flat as rollers above or below or both relentlessly tried to nudge the last ounce of excess fat from well-fed bodies. Some girls worked out on parallel bars, others swung from flying limbs. Amazon instructors, unsentimental as Parris Island drill sergeants, bullied doll-faced maidens into repeated vaults and turns on leather horses.

Flint could not allow himself either aesthetic or simple masculine pleasure in his spying. As soon as he was sure that Terry, Denise and Jan were not among the gym crowd, he went on, stooping under windows, until he found an unlocked door.

He pushed it open and tiptoed into the main entrance of the section to which the girls had been consigned only hours before. An anteroom in tasteful gray and white marble led to the main vault area, a large cruciform room with a marble scroll, lettered in gold, above its gateway: "CRYOBIOLOGY: THE MODERN WAY TO ETERNAL LIFE."

Row on row of glassed-in cubicles stretched the whole length back. As Flint watched, the lighting of the vault area brightened, but he held his position at the anteroom gate without moving, concentrating on the network of slender glass tubes and insulated wires which ran from each box to central temperature control and special fluid- and humidity-control storage banks in the side walls.

The increased light revealed more than tubes and wires. Now Flint could see that most of the cubicles were occupied by women. The women were as rigid and motionless as store-window mannequins and they wore as varied an assortment of attire. Here was a young woman in evening dress, next to her a swingy teenager in a miniskirt, further on down a top-flight lady executive in a cocktail suit, her face immobilized in a pensive expression as if she were deciding whether to paint an entire airline puce or pistachio.

The two cubicles farthest from him, Flint noted, were rimed with an opaque coating of whitish frost. So the cryobiology procedure must be to fill from the far end . . .

Lisa Norton, smiling on the success of her silent entry, cleared her throat.

Flint, without starting in reaction, turned his head toward her.

"I imagine," Lisa said through her smile, "you will find it all a bit, ah, Gothic?" Her hand indicated the vaults and their frozen contents. "What must you think of us, coming into Fabulous Face in this way, by the back door, so informally, I mean?"

Flint matched her casualness.

"But not so unexpectedly, I gather," he said, smiling. "Is all of this real? Cryobiology?"

"Quite real," Lisa said. "We call it the 'save-for-later program.' Here, people worth keeping may be preserved for a time more worth living in. As a matter of fact, Mr. Flint, isn't it the ultimate luxury? To suspend Time for as long as you wish? To return fifty, a hundred years later—"

"To be quick-frozen in nitrogen gas and thawed out some time later like a supermarket pizza is not precisely the classical idea of immortality," Flint said. He gestured at the two most heavily frosted cubicles. "What about those two? Occupied?"

Lisa nodded.

"Br-r-r-r!" Flint shivered.

"Frankly, I think it's a bit far out myself," Lisa said. "But one can't stand in the way of progress."

She linked a slim hand on Flint's arm. Dawdling in the Cryobiology Room exchanging cocktail party chit chat was not part of her strategy at a time when minutes counted.

"But this isn't much of a welcome or much of a tour," she said, steering him toward a staircase exit. "Let's go up by the pool. I'm sure many of our ladies are dying to catch a glimpse of the famous Derek Flint."

"You're very flattering." Flint let himself be led. "But there are a few matters, urgent matters, that I'd like to attend to. Besides, you haven't told me anything about—"

"Your harem," Lisa broke in with a liquid laugh. "That is, your *staff*. Why, I assumed you knew. They left just this morning."

They had reached the top of the stairs. Lisa locked the Cryobiology door behind her and promenaded Flint along a terrace. Guests of the resort, sipping drinks and chatting, raised heads to watch the handsome couple. Some made audible comments on Flint, the only man to be seen within the purlieus of Fabulous Face.

"Some hunk of . . ."

"I'd been wondering what it was I missed. Now I begin to remember."

"Gorgeous!"

"Tough!"

"Like mother used to make."

Lisa was as conscious as Flint of the well-matched couple they made, but she felt constrained to mock the admiration of her weaker sisters.

"You're accustomed to adulation from women," she said. "But to me, all those sickly sighs are—" She groped for proper condemnation.

"Ridiculous," Flint supplied. "You're quite right, Miss Norton. It's a relief to be with a beautiful woman who's superior to that sort of thing."

Lisa felt a moment's vulnerability.

"I never suggested that I—" She stopped when she saw Flint's widening smile.

"Oh, you really are good at it, aren't you?" she said with an edge of venom. "Tell me, Mr. Flint, what is this marvelous male superiority that captivates women?"

They had passed to a deserted section of the terrace, and the tropic moon, a rich, creamy white and full, cast snake shadows from the iron filigree work of the railing. A scent of jasmine whispered through the bougainvilleas. From far below came the rhythmic tinkle of a native band in the village.

Flint smiled down at Lisa.

"The secret is very simple," he said. "I don't compete with them."

She turned her face upward without any volition. The night, the moon, the scent, the music and Flint blended together. Any other action was impossible.

Flint's face met hers, slowly and gently at first, and then into a kiss that was long and demanding. Lisa Norton did not pull away. When Flint raised his head, her arms were still around him.

"There," he said. "That ends the suspense."

The candid honesty of his remark stopped Lisa in her first impulse to protest and rail.

"You're quite right," she admitted. "I was curious."

She looked up again at the long, proud face above hers, lines of experience and a kind of wisdom carving its cheeks.

"And now you've had the tour and so have I," she said, glancing at her watch. "And it's getting late." She became businesslike. "Shall I have someone drive you to the airport?"

"No, thank you," Flint said. "I'm not leaving just yet, you see."

He looked down at Lisa, and now his eyes were very cool and intent.

"Where are the girls?" he asked.

Lisa fluttered her augmented eyelashes in sweet innocence.

"Why, they left this morning," she said. "I told you, didn't I?"

"I don't think they did," Flint said, "since you so obviously expected me. And I'd also like to know a little more about the two cosmonauts."

"Two cosmonauts?" Lisa employed her eyelashes again. "Really, Mr. Flint, I don't follow your—"

"Natasha told me everything," Flint said bluntly. "In Moscow, just yesterday. But I need a few additional answers to fill in—"

This time Lisa cut Flint off, not by conversation, but by snapping her fingers. From the darkness bordering the terrace came four Amazon guards, none of them less than five feet nine inches of superbly shaped muscularity.

Flint crouched automatically to a judo defense stance. Then, noting the sex of his opponents, he shrugged and straightened up.

Lisa's smile had a flavoring of disappointment. She might have enjoyed a brannigan in which the male heroics of the famous Flint were worsted by her distaff warriors.

"I'm glad to see you're running true to form," she said. "Our reports mentioned that this kind of silly gallantry was your chief—vice."

"One of my worst," Flint admitted, bowing gallantly at the four Amazons. "Lead on, ladies."

Bewildered, the super-girl guards looked to Lisa for instructions.

"I think we'd better take him to the office," she decided. "Two in front of him, two behind."

She led the procession.

"Follow me, Mr. Flint," she said, poise recovered. "The additional answers you may find here will all come too late."

8

Desks had been removed from the penthouse central office. Fabric samples, fashion sketches, consumer-preference charts, automotive designs, architectural drawings had all vanished.

The room now resembled, more than anything else, a major political-party headquarters confidently awaiting word of landslide victory on election night. Long tables flanked the side walls, each bearing constantly emptied and replenished IN and OUT baskets. Lady executives barked and snarled into multiple telephone sets. Trim, younger girls wearing modified WAAC uniforms moved up and down the aisles with messages, fresh coffee pots, whispered orders and counterorders.

The focal point of the room was its end wall, where two TV monitors on either side of a large countdown clock transmitted information on the latest launching. Despite the ceaseless activity in the room, every eye strayed back to the monitor screens, and to the moving hands of the clock. As morning sunlight began to slant through the slatted windows, the clock read: 3 : 38.

A disembodied voice boomed from behind the monitors: "Start range read-out of PCM telemetry."

Women in officers' uniforms made notations on graph-paper pads.

"Range read-out," another ghostly voice answered. "Roger."

Pencils raced, WAAC runners fed information-punched cards into squat computers.

At the Command end of the room, directly under the clock and monitors, Elizabeth, Helena and Simone worked at their own tables. One empty table in the middle was reserved for Lisa.

"Is the Cleveland Group ready?" a lady colonel asked Helena.

"All in order," Helena said. The colonel saluted and went back to her own table. Helena was already listening to a radiotelephone communication from Ankara.

"Canada seems unsure of the proper parliamentary procedure, Miss Simone," an officer questioned.

"Switch them through to Iris in London," Simone said, not looking away from the monitors. "She has all the Commonwealth data ready and computed."

A worried general rapped on Helena's table.

"Miss Li fears reprisals from the Red Guards if we use Plan D in Peking."

"Tell her to check the correspondence," Helena said. "We covered that whole problem in File 37-P-4682a."

Elizabeth hushed a crowd of arguing military and civilian aides around her.

"Let's not have that media discussion all over again," she chided. "The announcement will have to be on television at the same time everywhere."

"But the different time zones—"

"I *know* people will be sleeping in Hawaii," Elizabeth raised her voice in lost patience, "but the timing has to be exactly on the button everywhere. For psychological impact—"

She stopped and pointed a lacquered nail at the monitor.

A genuine WAAC appeared on the screen, entering the Control Room at the launching site, distributing papers among the N.A.S.A. and Z.O.W.I.E. dignitaries. As the WAAC reached the center of the room, on full camera, she paused just a moment and brushed her hair twice with her right hand

"That's the signal!" Helena purred.

"The actor is on stage," Elizabeth said contentedly.

"Exactly on schedule," Simone said. "Marvelous."

The Countdown Clock rested a few minutes, then started into motion again.

"Verify all airborne hatches and doors are secure," the mysterious monitor voice spoke its gobblydegook message of space jargon.

Outside the penthouse door, Flint picked up the message and stopped. The Amazons bumped pleasantly at his rear.

"The office is right through there," Lisa prompted, jerking her thumb impatiently at the door.

Flint looked back and checked his directional bearings without hurry.

"It was the long climb up," he said. "I thought you girls seemed a bit winded."

"Oh, no," the lead Amazon assured him. "We're in great shape. If you could see how we train—"

"I'd love to," Flint said. "How many push-ups—"

"Stop it, girls!" Lisa commanded. The Amazons subsided, blushing through their even tan.

"You never quit, do you?" Lisa sneered at Flint. "It can't help you here. Come on. They're waiting."

The lead Amazon pushed open the door and Flint and Lisa made their entrance.

Elizabeth, Helena and Simone, attentive to the monitors at their end of the room, did not at first notice the ripple of excitement caused by Flint's arrival. Otherwise disciplined feminine heads swiveled from paper work and computer chores to observe the tall, saturnine agent's casual walk down the center aisle. Little girl-to-girl whispers replaced the efficient hubbub of before.

"The one they've been talking about . . ."

"The one with the girls?"

"Craggy, but cute."

"Aren't his eyes a little close together?"

"A perfect house pet, if he could be tamed."

The change in the rhythm of the room penetrated to the monitor end. Elizabeth, Helena and Simone turned to see Flint and Lisa.

Whispers died away. There was a bounded segment of silence while the three women gauged the quality of their notable adversary. Flint, candid and well-bred as ever in his bearing, made his own observations.

Lisa ushered him forward and broke the ice.

"This, of course, is Derek Flint," she said, as if the busy, businesslike room were a garden-party gala. "Miss Helena, Miss Elizabeth, Miss Simone."

Flint accepted each proffered hand with a courtly bow and a murmured acknowledgement.

"Charmed."

"Such a pleasure."

"My privilege."

Elizabeth looked at him appraisingly, hiding neither curiosity nor surprise.

"You seem younger than I'd imagined," she said. "To have made all those swashbuckling films so long ago, I mean."

Flint puckered his brow in polite confusion.

Lisa and the other two leading ladies giggled at an error typical of Elizabeth's other-worldliness.

"You're thinking of a man named Flynn, Miss Elizabeth," Lisa explained. "The actor. This is Derek Flint, the—ah—"

"The tourist," Flint rescued her quickly. "I think that would cover me. But I *do* recognize all of *you.*"

His smile was flattery, but informed flattery, the best grade.

"Publishing," he went on, "fashions, cosmetics, communications—you're famous ladies. What you don't manage directly, you control, and what you don't control, you influence, and what you don't influence, you'll probably eventually inherit."

Elizabeth was the first to respond.

"That's very well put," she said. "Don't you agree, girls?"

"Our Mr. Flint has always been noted for succinct and telling analysis," Lisa said. Helena and Simone granted curiously girlish and engaging grins of agreement. There was in the air an incongruous after-you-my-dear-Alphonsine conviviality. Flint seemed on the verge of another series of bows, but the monitor interrupted him.

"Verify ambient tests and range read-outs are complete and are satisfactory."

The mangled English of the monitor voice broke the spell completely.

The room returned to its activity and Lisa and her friends looked back toward monitors and the Countdown Clock.

"Seeing all of you here together is quite a sight for a mere man," Flint spoke above the hubbub. "A kind of summit conference of brains and beauty. But what is the topic of the meeting?"

No one gave answer.

"Here you sit," Flint completed his own problem, "watching a rocket. So that rocket holds the answer to everything. But what?"

The Alert Light beneath the Countdown Clock blinked on with a red glow.

"The women cosmonauts," Flint said, holding up one finger, "whom you put into space." He held up another finger. "The space platform, which is in your control."

"He's really very clever," Simone praised, a schoolmistress complimenting a backward but promising male child.

"Natasha talked to him," Lisa cut in. "How much, I don't know, but she talked."

"Did she now?" Helena digested the data. "Did you hurt her, Mr. Flint?"

Flint's bland, tomcat smile was a volume of answers.

"No, I see," Helena said. "You're quite a fellow. No wonder your girls were so hard to convince."

"I'd like to be sure they're all right," Flint said. "May I see them?"

"I told you they went home," Lisa said.

"No," Flint sighed. "We all know better than that. And I judge by the clock that time is getting short. Please, ladies, don't force me to use violence."

The Amazon guard detail, which had kept several paces to the rear, stepped closer.

"No, girls," Elizabeth halted them. "That won't be necessary. Your, ah, family is fine, Mr. Flint. They will come to no harm. We are simply saving them for later, keeping them on ice, as it were."

Flint's cheek muscles moved in an involuntary shiver.

"I see you know," Helena said. "I hope the knowledge may ensure your good behavior."

"The cubicles in the far corner downstairs?" Flint looked to Lisa and she shrugged assent. "Very efficient. And the sudden discrediting of Mr. Cramden? That, too, would have been your work—"

"The pad is open for essential personnel," graveled the monitor voice.

Elizabeth picked up a pencil and made a check on the schedule sheet on her table.

"He is clever indeed," she said, "but it's getting late and there's lots to do. Go away, Mr. Flint. By this time tomorrow all your questions will be answered. As soon as Project Damocles is complete, we can have a nice long talk."

"Damocles!" Flint raised his head like a hunting dog scenting his real quarry. "Damocles? That's not possible. The Damocles Plan calls for nuclear weapons to be used as a threat. It's a completely discredited idea. No man in his right mind would—"

"No man," Simone chuckled. "Quite right, Mr. Flint."

"You see?" Lisa said, no longer amused. "We can't let him free even here, much less leave."

"Quite right, dear," Elizabeth concurred. "Don't be so fretful, Mr. Flint. By this time tomorrow women will be running the world and you'll see how quickly things will settle down to better than normal."

"Running the world?" Flint showed naked surprise for one of the first times in his long career of facing the fantastic. "But, dear ladies, you can't be serious. How would you—"

"How would we what?" Elizabeth snapped. "Do the work? How many businesses are actually being run by secretaries, mistresses, wives? If the boss goes away for a few days, a few weeks, does the work stop?"

"That's probably true," Flint conceded, "but still I can't imagine how—"

"You can't imagine how we poor dear ladies hope to cope with it all?" Simone broke in with icy sarcasm. "Face it, Mr. Flint. We women are outliving you right now. The wealth of this country and the world is being concentrated in our dishpan hands. In laboratory and factory our reflexes are faster than yours, our manual dexterity twenty per cent higher and our patience a damned sight longer. There's nothing we have to prove. It's all been proven already and its down in black and white on the records for anyone with an eye to read."

Flint nodded patiently.

"Granting all that," he said, "what's your hurry? You have only to wait and it will all fall into your laps. You will still have laps when you're wearing pants, I assume."

"I gather you are not too impressed with our plans?" Lisa spoke up.

"But of course I'm impressed," Flint said. "It's just that it seems a bit farfetched to me. After all, there are millions of women all over the world who might not see things your way."

"Millions?" Elizabeth raised her eyebrows. "I wonder . . ."

She motioned to one of the Amazons.

"Show Mr. Flint how the dryer works, Shelley," she ordered. "Go ahead and inspect it, Mr. Flint. I'm sure you will be interested."

Flint followed the Amazon noncom across to a table behind which stood a cluster of Fabulous Face dryers. Two of the girl guards had already responded to Elizabeth's order by stripping the outer plastic shell from one model.

Flint picked it up and held it closer. He saw a miniature tape system concealed in the otherwise normal thermal coils.

The Amazon sergeant pressed a small button and the tape mechanism started to spin slowly with a very faint hum. Flint held it to his ear.

". . . asked yourself why Marcia lives with a clod like John, or even why Juliet suffered over an oaf like

Romeo? And how about you? Every day in every way you see the evidence that Man is the hitchhiker and Woman is the driver, designer, mechanic, anything else you can name. Think it over the next night you're lying awake next to that snoring, rumpled, spoiled and babyish lump of a husband or lover who thinks the world owes him a living, the world and you, my dear. Think it over and think what you and every other woman might do about it. Two thousand years ago, Aristophanes wrote . . ."

He put the tiny speaker with its soft, convincing, honeyed voice back down on the table.

"I suppose when the hair is wet, the current is conducted and the programming is received almost unconsciously," he thought aloud. "Brain- and hair-washing at the same time. Do you really think you can get away with it?"

"Get away with it?" Elizabeth looked at Flint almost in pity. "Mr. Flint, think a minute. Dryers like these have been around for some time. Right? Well, for many years now, every time a woman went into a beauty shop she came out a bit more dissatisfied with a man's world. A student of such things would notice that the beauty parlor in its modern sense and the unhappy modern woman arrived at about the same time. We've been busy, Mr. Flint. The contented housewife is a thing of the past. And the future—the future is ours!"

"Quite an idea," Flint murmured. And then, crisply, he said, "Ladies, I'm sure your facts are accurate. But like every other underdog in the world, you know more about the illness than the cure. Now what you propose merely turns the coin over. It's still the same old coin. If it's a slug on one side it's a slug on the other side. Forget it!"

The rebel leaders studied him with varying expressions of amusement and unbelief. When he reached to pick up an intercom speaker from the table, the Amazons were at his elbow.

They were, as has been noted, exceedingly robust girls. They outnumbered Flint and, at these close quarters, they had a better than even chance to overwhelm him by sheer weight.

But the interesting struggle never began. A loud commotion filled the hall at the other end of the room. The door burst open, and there in the doorway stood General Carter and a dozen burly soldiers, disheveled but victorious over the portal-guarding Amazons who had tried to bar their way.

"General Carter!" Elizabeth screamed. "What is the meaning of this? Why aren't you with Sebastian getting the flight ready? You know what your instructions were!"

Carter swaggered up the aisle and pushed Elizabeth into a chair.

"Shut up and sit down, Your Highness," he advised unnecessarily. "Little girls' playtime is over."

Helena made an indignant gesture and Carter cuffed her, too, into a seat. Lisa and Simone took the hint and sat down quietly.

"I bet you've been getting an earful of this malarkey, too," Carter leered confidentially at Flint. Flint had had a moment's hope at the General's first apearance, but exposure to the naked power-lust written on his features killed any such optimism.

"Well, forget it, all of you." Carter wheeled to address the whole room. "The situation is well in hand. *Our* hand." He made a mocking half-bow to the lady leaders. "Did you really think we were going to go through all that just for you old broads?"

Helena brushed her forehead with a helpless hand, close to the femininity of tears.

"Come on now, did you?" Carter sneered.

"But Sebastian Trent believed in us," Simone said. "And you did, too. And the girls on the space platform."

"Sebastian Trent!" Flint muttered recognition. "One of the world's great actors."

"The best!" Carter said. "He took you all in, didn't he? You know something? He's really enjoying being the President. We just might make the whole deal permanent."

"But all that time," Elizabeth said brokenly, fighting against acceptance. "The years involved in the planning. He couldn't have fooled us. He was so sincere."

"He was sincere all right," Carter said. "So was I. But that was before we saw the view from the top."

"He was good enough to fool Cramden and everyone else," Flint admitted.

"We were fools to trust any man," Elizabeth said hollowly.

"It was a magnificent job of plastic surgery." Flint looked to Helena. "Your work?"

"Thank you," Helena said. "But wasted, all wasted now."

Carter signaled to his squad.

"I hate to break this up," he said, "but I'm going to have to be there when the balloon goes up." He waved at the monitors. "Tie all the dames up nice and snug and take this batch down to the freezer." His last gesture encompassed Flint, Lisa, Helena, Simone and Elizabeth.

"What about Cramden and the real President?" an aide asked.

"Relax," Carter snorted. "Lloyd C. Cramden and the thirty-ninth President of these United States are in the deep freeze already."

Flint winced.

"Worried about your pal?" Carter asked with fake solicitude. "Don't worry, we'll see him in a minute, fresh as Atlantic City seafood. Get moving, men. Take them down to the freezer and put them away."

The handful of Amazon guards who had accompanied Flint and Lisa into headquarters stirred toward action, but Lisa sadly shook her head at them. Twice their number would have been no match for Carter's hand-picked personal squad of heavily armed bully boys.

Carter directed his men out the doorway, the last rank moving backwards, alert to any possible revolt.

"Good show!" Carter rasped—and Flint, as if the words were the signal of overconfidence he had been awaiting, gave his hoarse karate cry. Then he leaped over the heads of his guards and raced down the darkened staircase.

"Hey!" Carter shouted. "Nail him, boys!"

One of his élite guard raised a carbine but Carter, seeing the shadows of other troops spilling into the path below, knocked it down before he could fire.

"Catch him, dammit!" he roared. "Don't just spray everybody in sight."

Flint had a good lead now, beyond the first reinforcements and down to the path skirting the beach. He loped along the path, only to find two of Carter's men waiting by the stairs that linked the patio to the dryer area.

Impatient at the delay, Flint made only seconds' work of felling one into the knees of the other, aiding the second man's stumble with a sharp hand-cut to his neck.

He crossed the patio, past knots of bewildered and cowering women, some guests at Fabulous Face, some employees. He sprinted to the gym, where he had first come into the resort.

Behind him he could hear an occasional cry from some woman, the deeper, harsher barked orders of Carter and his gang.

He swung open a door and darted into the gym. He hoped for at least temporary sanctuary on its upper level, but again he found two men already on hand to upset his plans. One of them gave a view halloo and the other headed for the stairs leading to Flint's balcony.

Flint flexed his leg muscles. He let his pursuers get better than halfway up the stairs, then dived from the balcony to the exercise floor below.

Those women who had been caught in the gym by Carter's lightning coup d'état set up high shrieks at this new development. They huddled together, sheeplike, blocking the two guards who were trying to capture Flint, but at the same time forming a squirming wall of feminine flesh between Flint and his possible escape route. As the guards elbowed a rough path through them, the women took advantage of the opened door to straggle out to freedom.

Flint, with the first guard already running to butt him head first in the belly, could only envy them silently as he caught the man's head before it connected, raised a knee to his midriff and tumbled him back. The man fell, dazed, onto a canvas mat, but his companion sidestepped him and charged at Flint, sawing the air with a heavy MP's truncheon.

Flint knelt and jumped. He caught the flying rings above him and swung through the air to a safe spot. But now the first guard, recovered, was lunging toward him.

There was a longhorse at the side of the gym and between them. Flint took a running lead toward it, touched it with one outstretched hand for leverage, and landed feet first on the unprotected chest of his opponent. The man went down and Flint's eyes darted around the gym for a window, a door, an air duct, any exit.

There was nothing immediately visible save the door and Flint's path was blocked by the second guard, a hirsute Neanderthal with family resemblances to both King Kong and a Kodiak bear. Kong moved with a speed and agility unusual to such bulk. In two steps he had Flint in a massive, bone-cracking hug. Flint punched at chest and shoulders and face, but the blows brought no reaction beyond an ominous chuckle.

Kong carried Flint like an unruly child and set him down on a rowing machine. He leaned down to grip Flint for another hug, but Flint, in that scant moment of freedom, grabbed the rowing machine arms and stroked back like a Kelly at Henley. The first stroke took him out of Kong's reach. A second stroke sent the oar arms smashing one into each ankle of the hairy guard.

The tactic slowed Kong enough for Flint to get to his feet, but the guard came on, trapping Flint against the wall next to a complicated roller-massage machine.

He reached to clutch Flint in a final, lethal hug.

Flint reached above his head and pulled a lever. The machine rumbled into action, front and back rollers swinging into position around the guard. Flint then adjusted the controls to keep Kong in a reducing massage indefinitely.

He had disposed of Kong just in time. The first guard was coming back, weaving with sinister care toward Flint.

Flint's breath came in painful gulps. He knew himself to be momentarily unfit for hand-to-hand combat, but his hand happened to brush a push-button container of hair spray left by one of the guests. He caught it up forthwith and squirted it into the oncoming guard's eyes.

A muffled, frustrated scream burst from the guard's throat. He clawed at his eyes. Flint hoisted him onto a nearby exercycle, fixed his hands on the handlebars and set the machine to top speed.

Flint's breathing was still labored, but he took time out to glance behind him as he went out the door. The gym was deserted save for the two guards. The hairy Kong kept clawing with muffled animal shouts at the smooth rubber rollers that encased him in a living, massaging cage, while his buddy bent helpless over the whirring exercycle, his knees jiggling up and down and up and down at a speed so frenzied that he was afraid to take a hand away from the grips to turn down the speed.

"Keep in training, boys!" Flint waved a casual hand in farewell.

Reassuring quiet reigned outside the gym. Flurried females had fled to their rooms. Flint could see no lurking figures, innocent or threatening, between himself and the corridor leading to the Cryobiology Storage vaults. And there, whatever the peril within, was where Flint had to go. He checked his equipment and found it in order. He could only hope it would suffice against any further threats.

He squared his shoulders, dusted some dirt from his jacket and opened the Cryobiology gates.

"Everyone's been waiting for you, Flint," General Carter said smoothly.

"Sorry I was late," Flint said even more smoothly as Carter's bodyguards stepped warily from either side to hem him in. "I just can't seem to get through a day without my little workout."

He went along without resistance as Carter and his goon squad shepherded Lisa, Helena, Simone and Elizabeth and himself into the vault room. The silent rows of glassed-in semimortal icicles seemed to demand an awed silence. Flint promptly broke it.

"Seems an elaborate form of murder." He frowned at two cubicles containing handsome young women in evening dress.

"Murder?" Carter bridled. "It's rather humane. By freezing all of you and keeping you at the temperature of liquid oxygen, we keep you in perfect condition. No exposure to all the nasty germs of the outside atmosphere. Hundreds of thousands of dollars' worth of precision equipment working night and day all for you."

He sounded like a star salesman for a retirement village.

"Decent of you," Flint agreed.

"Oh, I'm more considerate than you think," Carter said. "Nothing I like better than making everybody happy—within reasonable bounds of security, of course."

He looked from Flint to the leaders of the feminist world revolution.

"Like right now," he said. "Since there aren't enough freezers to go around, you'll all just have to double up. And I'll see to it, Flint, that you have a lovely companion." He hooked a vulgar thumb at Lisa. "Hey?"

One of his minions caught Lisa's arms up behind her and thrust her next to Flint.

"I realize," Carter smirked, "at a reunion like this there's quite a bit you'd like to say to each other, but there's not much time left in the old ball game."

Lisa ground her teeth in frustration. Flint remained calmly silent.

The guards bundled Helena and Elizabeth together and shoved them into the first empty cubicle. Flint felt the first blast of arctic air even before the glass door closed on its airproof rubber insulating bands.

Simone was given the honor of a vault to herself.

Flint and Lisa found themselves in the last empty freezing chamber. Lisa's teeth were already chattering. Carter turned the last oxygen valve himself, and waved a contemptuous farewell.

His men closed the area door behind them. The first particles of ice began to form about Flint's ankles as they left.

A superpowered speedboat was waiting on the Fabulous Face beach. The boat picked up Carter and his élite guard. It churned phosphorescence from blue-green water, cleaving its way across the island waters to the launching site.

In the disrupted HQ room of the penthouse, bound and gagged second-level executives of the Fabulous Face International watched gloomily as the activity on the monitor screens increased, and the Countdown Clock hands moved relentlessly onward.

"All systems at Go!" the monitor voice announced sepulchrally to the half-empty room.

Flint counted under his breath, the whispered words chattering in the cold, against the few minutes he knew it took for full refrigeration to set in.

"One ch-ch-chimpanzee, two ch-ch-ch-chimpanzees, three ch-ch-ch-ch-ch-ch . . ." He gave up keeping track of seconds to concentrate on the agonized effort to keep motion in his congealing wrist muscles, to move his hands to his belt buckle in time to stave off total disaster for the world, for his President, for Lloyd Cramden, for his girls, and for that matter, Lisa and Helena and Elizabeth and Simone.

The slightest movement sent dozens of small, razor-sharp knife pains through his hands and lower arms. The pains stabbed all the way up to the shoulder muscles that helped direct the motions, through his neck, into his cold-drowsed brain. Beads of perspiration formed by the effort froze at once and fell with dull tinkles to the floor of the cubicle.

The belt buckle was his only hope. His fingers reached it and then, when pain and effort became too great, they fell away a half-inch that took miles to regain.

His tight-clamped lips felt a film of thin ice building where saliva had escaped.

He made his fingers move again. They just touched the buckle, and for an unholy instant Flint had to struggle to remember why on earth, why on ice the buckle had any importance. Then his mind flickered back to action. In a final spasm his fingers released the hidden tuning fork. His thumb spasm struck it and a clear, high, soundless note rang out. Then came the clatter of breaking glass.

Flint pitched forward. He broke his fall with one rigid arm, and broke Lisa's following fall with his body.

He forced himself to roll free of the cold air from the broken cubicle. He lay still for ten deep breaths. At last he felt circulation returning to his limbs.

He rose quickly, pulled Lisa to her feet, and slapped her cheeks gently until she recovered.

The next ten minutes were all speed and efficiency. Lisa managed the freezer controls, shutting off the liquid-oxygen flow while Flint bashed open vault after vault—Cramden, the President, Denise, Helena, Jan, Terry, Simone, Elizabeth.

When this essential personnel had been liberated Flint hushed their note-comparing.

"We all know the situation now," he said. "The countdown is just an hour away."

"What's the use?" Cramden wailed, still shivering. "There's no way of getting there in time."

"A call from you, Mr. President," Flint spoke to

Melvin Muffly. "There's an airbase right next to Fabulous Face."

"Who'd believe me?" the President wondered.

"They *can't* be allowed to succeed," Flint said firmly.

"But they took the boat," Elizabeth said. "How do we get to launching site?"

"When I came in," Flint said, "I passed a lot of stuff on your beach that would float. I understand your staff is very athletic?"

"I don't understand," Elizabeth confessed.

"I do," Lisa joined in excitedly. "And we *can*. I'll get the girls and meet you on the beach. Look, Miss Elizabeth." She paused with love and sympathy for her old comrade in arms. "Our way just didn't work. We've got to team up with these—men."

"But what can we do when we get there?" Elizabeth asked.

"The old standby," Lisa said. "OPERATION SMOOCH."

"OPERATION SMOOCH!" Flint picked up the phrase with satisfaction. "Let's go!"

9

OPERATION SMOOCH began as a tropical Dunkirk in reverse.

Lisa had gathered together the loyal and revivified members of the Amazon guard and led them to the beach area, where Flint and the others were busily at work securing any and all floatable objects. Flint blessed the lavish hand with which Fabulous Face had been furnished for every water pleasure. There were pedal-boats and plastic kayaks, surfboards of all sizes, sea sleds, styrofoam and kapok rafts, a scattering of fabulous sea monsters in inflated rubber.

The three largest rafts Flint reserved for command parties: the President, Cramden, Lisa and himself in one; Denise, Jan and Terry in another; Simone, Elizabeth and Helena in the third; each large raft with four bikinied Amazons for kick-power motorization. Lisa, familiar with her own chain of command, split up the smaller transport into squads under command of trusted aides such as Hilda.

When the full array was ready at the shoreline, each float loaded and manned, or womanned, Flint raised his hand and let it fall in a "forward" signal.

From one end to the other, the beach came alive. Craft nosed into the shallow surf and, as soon as swimming depth was reached, well-muscled bronzed legs kicked foam high. The colorful, absurd armada entered Caribbean waters and headed toward the key launching area.

In the balcony of the rocket central control room,

Melvin-Sebastian Trent-Muffly stood beside his trusted military and security chief, General David Carter, and smugly watched the activity in the room below them. Visiting foreign dignitaries, scientists and uniformed liaison officers from England, France, Japan, Italy and a dozen other powers, watched with them as the Count-down Clock crept past 30 : 00 to 29 : 00 and on.

All eyes were on the details of the launching. No one was curious or frivolous enough to observe the multi-colored and strangely swift fleet coming into the bay beyond the launching area.

Flint sat erect on his raft, directing the forward progress of the armada with gestures, looking back with satisfaction at the even, steady and attractive motion of dozens of pairs of brown legs behind every float.

In Control Central the clock read 27 : 00.

Flint got his first wave ashore. They advanced into a densely wooded area of palms and undergrowth next to the missile complex.

Hilda, beach captain for the remaining floats, waved them to a beach point nearby.

"Start tank sensor checks," the briefing officer spoke into the monitor system mike.

"You know the terrain, sir." Flint let Cramden take the lead from the wooded rendezvous point to the thick hedge circling the missile complex.

Behind Flint and Cramden crept their raggle-taggle army of liberation. President Muffly, some of his dignity regained, walked arm in arm with Elizabeth, Lisa came close on Flint's heels, Simone and Helena accompanied Denise, Terry and Jan. The husky Amazons led the rest with the sure skill of Commando training. They moved in a broken line, taking shelter in shadow and vegetation on the way.

Blocked by the thick hedge, Flint tugged at a heavy camouflage net, but found it firmly anchored.

"Your people did a good job here, sir," he complimented Cramden.

"Thank you," Cramden said, searching his memory

for the original security blueprints. "We try." He pointed to another net section to the right. "I think if we pull this one."

He and Flint tugged together. The net slipped aside and unveiled an opening to the missile sites. Through it Flint could see cleverly camouflaged low domes blending into the tropic landscape. Armed-guard details dotted the area, the largest cluster concentrated at the main entrance to the most monumental of the domes.

"That's it, sir?" Flint asked.

Cramden nodded.

An officer at the main-dome entrance picked up binoculars to focus at the disturbance caused by movement of the net. He called out an order and a squad of guards wheeled from the dome and advanced at a dog trot, rifles carried at the ready.

"We're sunk," Cramden whispered. "And so close . . ."

Lisa was whispering her own suggestions into Flint's other ear, pointing to the bikini Amazons lurking in the bushes.

"Our best bet," Flint whispered back. "Can they do it?"

"Poof!" Lisa whispered. "They've been doing it since adolescence."

She turned and signaled to Hilda, holding four fingers high.

"Tactic Four," Hilda relayed to an aide named Gretchen. "Come-and-Get-It."

"Come-and-Get-It," Gretchen relayed to Eloise the tape-checker.

"Good ol' Come-and-Get-It," Eloise told her girls.

Flint signaled for his forces to spread out. He pulled Cramden with him into denser cover and the President followed.

The first three guards came cautiously through the opening. They looked over the terrain before signaling their buddies to follow. Lisa, behind a thick palm, let the whole detail through before she waved back to Hilda.

"Hey!" the point-man cried out. "Wha!?!"

From a bush ten yards in front of him a tanned feminine arm was holding up the wispy bikini bandeau as a flag of surrender. Or truce. Or something.

"Hey!" his nearest buddy copied. Three more bikini tops had blossomed from the bushes ahead. And six more. And seven more.

And with the improvised flags sprouted their owners, lissome girls by the dozen, everyone as topless as the best businessman's lunch San Francisco could offer.

Bug-eyed, the troops of Z.O.W.I.E. let their rifles slump harmlessly as the girls moved toward them, hands raised in surrender, hips undulating promisingly. At contact point, the Fabulous Face Amazons turned on their judo training, and by then the guards were easy prey. Flint and Cramden joined in the final subduing of the dome detail, but their efforts were scarcely necessary.

The only surprise of the encounter belonged to Cramden.

Grabbing the officer in charge who had come to see what was happening to his detail, he found himself face to face with his aide, Avery.

"Thank God!" Avery cried as Cramden's hand poised to knock him out. "I've been expecting you, sir. There's no time to lose!"

Cramden gave him a quick bear-hug greeting.

"Mr. Flint, ladies," Avery assumed direction of a new force. "If you'll follow me, I can get you in."

Leaving the Z.O.W.I.E. guards stunned or trussed up or both, Flint and his very special forces followed Avery's lead into the missile complex. Entering the nearest dome, they filed down a long stairway and across an underground tunnel which connected to Control Central itself.

"Quietly now!" Avery warned at the rear entrance to

the sanctum of sanctums. "If you'll take over, Mr. Flint . . ."

Flint returned Avery's salute, then pressed his ear to the door. He could hear Sebastian Trent's superb impersonation of President Muffly taking in the foreign observers.

"Gentlemen," the rich voice intoned, "we are rapidly approaching what we hope will be the most momentous and meaningful launch of the century . . ."

"Now!" Flint directed in a low voice, passed along back down the corridor. "You first, Mr. President."

He opened the door on Trent's wind-up: "I'm sure you, as distinguished representatives of the governments who have sent you here, join me in wishing our two astronauts a smooth voyage and a successful link-up with the space platform which will circle eternally, not merely as a step toward further exploration but a living bond holding our own world ever more closely together in peace and cooperation."

"Bro-*ther!*" President Muffly sputtered as he led the way through the door.

A technician had been tabulating data at a table by the rear entrance. He started from his seat, looking goggle-eyed from Muffly to Trent.

"It's the President!" He stood at attention.

"The President!" A radio operator took up the cry and the confusion. "But who's that . . . ?"

Cramden's familiar bulk at the President's side mirrored a hundred familiar newspaper pictures and television frames. Flint, a pace behind, imitated the familiar and ubiquitous Secret Service guards. But nothing could explain the long tail of beautiful feminist leaders and neat (tops by now restored) Amazons.

"T-eight min-min-minutes," the countdown man stuttered, ending in a gasp: "The President! The Presidents?"

The space officials and guests in Control Central were not a mob of morons susceptible to panic when faced with the unexpected. The visiting military and diplomatic representatives were men who had faced down revolutions, soothed riots and negotiated with religious fanatics. The scientists, domestic and imported, were dedicated, if occasionally eccentric, individualists who, whatever their surface quirks, had exercised considerable self-control in the upward courses of their impressive careers. Even the lowliest of the guards had survived batteries of psychological tests for balance and dependability before being assigned to Z.O.W.I.E. One.

Thus there was no immediate chaos, but only a subdued muttering as Melvin Muffly, clothed in an interior real dignity beyond his sleep-creased golfing clothes, walked to the center of the room and leveled an accusing finger at the cut-awayed, stripe-trousered figure of Sebastian Trent on the balcony.

"Imposter!" Muffly said in a penetrating bellow.

Trent was an actor who had survived miscues, backstage accidents, garbled props and drunken leading ladies. Now he tried for an even measure of outraged dignity and righteous anger.

"It is you, sir, whoever you may be, who is an imposter!" he shouted back.

The murmurs of the crowd rose in volume. Eyes darted from Trent to Muffly. Whispered conversations touched upon shrillness.

Cramden stepped up next to the real President and waved arms agitatedly for silence.

"Quiet! Quiet, everyone!" he said commandingly. "I have an announcement to make."

"It's Cramden," a British aide whispered to a bemedaled Iranian Airforce general. "The Top Security Johnny."

*"Ex-*Top Security, cobber," a New Zealand colonel corrected.

"Been the President's right hand for years though," a Canadian said, thinking hard.

"Épatant!" General De Gaulle's representative shrugged at this latest example of Yankee confusion. *"Deux présidents!"*

"What you might call *embarras des riches,*" the Swedish nuclear expert agreed.

"Like too bloody much, man!" chimed in a gold-blanketed envoy from emerging Africa.

"Qui-et!" Cramden shouted again. He produced enough curiosity for most of the murmuring to die away.

"You all know me," Cramden said. "Right?"

There were "Yeses, *da's, oui's, ja's*" and a bobbing of nods.

"Most of you have known me for a good many years," he pressed his point. "Right?"

More audible assent. "Good old Lloyd!" said an Australian brigadier.

"OK," Cramden said, wheeling to point at Trent. "*That* man is the imposter."

Trent looked down from his balcony with the most confident and bland of smiles.

"Mr. Cramden is right," he said. "Ladies and gentlemen, I confess I was not elected to this office." A ripple of shock ran through his audience.

"I was not elected," he repeated coolly. "However, I do feel that there are compelling, indeed irresistible, reasons why I should continue in it."

Shock translated itself into vocal protest.

"I say, that's a bit thick!"

"Salaud!"

"Counterfeiter!"

Trent slapped a hand down on the balcony ledge. The sound rang through the room like a shot.

"General Carter!" he snapped.

Carter saluted neatly and gave a curt command to his élite guard. From the balcony, from the corners of the room, soldiers of the Trent-Carter régime leveled their weapons. Others moved out to disarm the few loyal troops, to replace some technicians with their own picked men.

General Carter, not a hair out of place on his thinning scalp, smiled down at his captive audience.

"The countdown will continue," he said. "The ol' ball game hasn't been called off. Just a seventh-inning stretch."

Lisa and Elizabeth winced at the dugout corn.

"I'll see that the bird flies right," Carter vowed to *his* President. To the countdown official: "Pick up that count, soldier."

He spun in an about-face and marched down the balcony with Major Cooper and his loyal dog-robber, Austin.

The countdown officer hesitated, turning to Cramden. A burly member of Carter's guard prodded him with a .45.

"T-Seven minutes," he spoke obediently into his mike.

Carter's picked men were working at their computers with concentrated efficiency. Except for the expressions of bewilderment on the faces of the foreign observers and the clear malevolence on the faces of Flint's party, it might have been any normal launching, with trained men and sophisticated machines teamed to do a history-making job of space exploration.

Trent smiled, taking a final look from the balcony before he turned to his armed guard to leave. As he passed a knot of international dignitaries, he stopped, overhearing comments no longer confined to whispers.

"Outrageous!"

"Charles always has said *jamais,* pardon me, never to trust *les américains."*

"Lodge immediate protests through the United Nations . . ."

"But Señor Lodge has resigned, no?"

"Don't be disturbed, gentlemen." Trent's reassurance had a second-layer of mockery. "I can promise you our relations with your governments will continue much as before." His smile was as comforting as a crocodile's. "In fact," he added, "with perhaps fewer disagreements."

Flint's eyes searched the Control Room for any vulnerable spot. A life history of tight squeezes made him believe that no security was ever airtight, but now he suspected that he had run into the rule-proving exception. Carter had deployed his forces with maximum efficiency. No loopholes were apparent even to Flint's trained inspection.

He groped in a pocket and pulled out his lighter. There might be a prayer, a faint chance of diversion, if he could activate the subminiature smoke-bomb mechanism.

"No gadgets, mac." A burly sergeant sighted his handgun at Flint's head.

"So sorry," Flint said, and replaced the last-chance lighter.

But Lisa's head was near his own.

"Whatever you have or think you have," Flint whispered, "it had better be soon."

Lisa's smile was that of a feminine sphinx.

"We still have *our* weapons," she whispered back. "We always do."

"And no small talk either," the sergeant said, shifting his aim to Lisa.

General Carter was partly visible on the monitor screen. Since there was no longer any need for secrecy, he had stepped into the astronauts' Ready Room.

The astronauts were fully suited and checked out for flight. They came to their feet and made the best salutes possible in their bulky garb.

Carter extended a hand for a farewell shake, caught the hand of the first astronaut returning his courtesy and flipped him to the floor with a judo tug. The guard at Carter's elbow felled the second astronaut with a brutal clunk of his rifle butt. He and another guard squatted to remove the space suits. The countdown continued to sound through the Control Room.

Lisa, unhurriedly, had moved next to Elizabeth and others of the Fabulous Face organization. She took one last glance at the Countdown Clock before whispering huskily: "OPERATION SMOOCH!"

Elizabeth weighed the idea for half a second, then nodded.

She and Lisa both turned casually toward the scattered Amazons and pursed their lips in a mimic kiss. All over the room, silently, girls made little kissing pouts back at them: rosebud lips, cupid's bows, lips pale with Tropic Ice lip-rouge, full lips, thin lips, red lips, pink lips and deep purple. The order had been given and received.

The average eye would have noted no change in the Control Room in the next few minutes. Aside from the technicians at their tasks, it was a nervous scene anyway and the slight movements of the scantily-clad Amazons seemed normal milling about as diplomats paced testily and guards shifted their posts to keep alert control. It could have been sheer coincidence that very quickly every soldier on guard duty had a girl either behind him, at his side, or in front of him.

Lisa gave the most imperceptible of nods.

A tall girl, who could have been posing for an ad headlined "I Dreamed I Was an Astronaut in My Maidenform Bra," nibbled gently at the earlobe of a guard lieutenant.

"I haven't seen a man in so long, honey," she cooed above her nibbling.

"I haven't seen a dame, either," the lieutenant said hoarsely. "Not one like you, baby." He found that his .45 was interfering with basic maneuvers and set it down on the table behind him.

"Love those butch-cuts," a compact model blonde husked, running massage-trained fingers through a sergeant's hair.

Slender arms snaked around a private's neck and tickled his chin.

"I adore whiskers!" confessed the 100-proof redhead at the other end of the arms.

"Whiskers adore you, doll," the soldier answered, kissing a soft palm.

A warm body, mostly bronzed skin enhanced by two

small bandanas, slipped onto the lap of the senior officer in charge.

"Hey!" he said, trying to tighten his grip on his automatic pistol.

"I can't help myself, sweetie, around a hunk of man like you," the bronzed beauty agonized.

"Who cares!" The officer deposited his gun on the floor and came to grips with his problem.

The technician in charge of the Countdown Clock let a limp hand fall from his control lever. A bird in the hand was worth two astronauts in outer space.

The sound of a solid, expertly delivered kiss popped through the room like the removal of a champagne cork. Every member of Carter's contingent, save only President-by-Chicanery Trent was being embraced by a lovely Amazon. Softer and louder pops echoed from all over.

"Verify range read-outs of launch vehicle—telemetry," rasped the monitor voice from the rocket site.

Nobody paid any mind.

"Baby, baby, you're killing me!" happily groaned a soldier from McKeesport, Pa.

"What the hell is this?" Trent came out of his bemused trance with a shout. "Sadie Hawkins Day? Break it up!"

"You ordered it, Trent!" Flint called gleefully. He and Cramden and Avery, with minor assistance from the President, major assistance from the judo squad of girls not actively engaged in the SMOOCH division of OPERATION SMOOCH, leaped into action.

In the missile Ready Room, General Carter made the last adjustments to the space suit he had taken from the first astronaut. The fit was perfect. He and Trent had been careful in maneuvering the astronaut selection procedure to ensure a good fit, and his hours of intensive study and practice left him feeling quite at home in the strange covering.

All the plans he and Trent had tacked on to the original Fabulous Face program were going smooth as butter. In a very short time they would control the whole Earth, more thoroughly and with a power a hundred times more awesome than any ancient conqueror from Alexander to Genghis Khan. With Trent a good ten years older than Carter, and in nowhere near the peak physical condition that the general had enforced upon himself from earliest sand-lot days, Carter's succession to supreme power was a lead-pipe cinch.

Little Davie Carter, who'd always just made the second eleven, the JV baseball team, perpetual runner-up, was going to be Captain of All Varsities.

But this was all future. The thing now was the present timing of the space shot.

Carter hulked his way into the elevator and was lifted to the capsule door.

Men cut off from feminine companionship and then suddenly offered a treat worthy of the more libidinous of naughty Roman Emperors were no match for Flint, Cramden, Avery, President Muffly and their Amazon allies. The battle, if it could be called that, ended almost as soon as it began. Disarmed soldiers sobbed with rage and frustration as they were snugly tied up and stacked out of the way in Control Central.

The foreign dignitaries assisted in the operation. Loyal technicians returned to their positions at computers and recording mechanisms.

Flint clamped a painful armlock on Trent and brought him to Cramden.

"Stop the countdown," Cramden ordered.

"Can't," Trent grunted. "Out of my hands now."

"Where's Carter?" Cramden barked.

"Where you can't touch him," Trent said defiantly. "In the capsule, if you want to know."

"Get him on the monitor," Cramden directed.

"I don't think that's possible," Trent sneered.

"Captain?" Cramden asked.

The monitor technician shook his head.

"The capsule connection is controlled from the other

end," he said. "You remember the Modesty Switch, sir?"

"Damn modesty!" Cramden railed. "Mr. President!"

Melvin Muffly looked up from the fascinating conversation he had been having with Lisa and her friends.

"Those hair dryers!" he was saying. "My own wife visits a beauty shop once a week. You mean to tell me . . . Yes, Lloyd?"

He twitched a little at the mirror image of Trent, held by Flint at Cramden's side.

"You, sir," he started to say, "whoever you are—"

His words were drowned in the keening of sirens and the frantic flashing of red alarm lights.

"Nuclear Alert!" Cramden cried. "Take shelter."

Bodies dodged to and fro, seeking the comfort of walls, crouching half under the stacks of trussed-up rebels. All but the hardiest technicians had left their posts.

"Sir," Cramden called the President's attention to the screen of the capsule monitor, slowly glowing to life. It blinked and then came to clear focus. A space-suited Carter was in his seat in the armed rocket.

"This is General Carter," his voice boomed through the disorderly room. "I've been tuned in on you for the past few minutes." His hand strayed down to the red lever that stuck up from the capsule floor like an antique gearshift.

"As you know," he said, "this lever controls the arming of ten megatons. An explosive force equal to ten million tons of TNT. Enough power to destroy the whole Caribbean area with a radiation fallout that could blanket half the world. I'm not mentioning earthquakes, tidal floods, fire storms and other minor incidentals. I know you don't want me to put this into operation."

Flint turned over Trent to a statuesque but muscular brunette.

"Keep him talking," he whispered to Cramden and the President. "Stall. I'm going after him."

"No, Flint!" Cramden begged. He turned to the President. "We've got to get people out of here, sir," he said. "Any delay and—"

"You're right, sir," Flint said grimly. "Any delay and we'll have no chance at all."

"Mr. President," Cramden's voice broke. "Order Flint not to try any nonsense. He's a reckless man, sir!"

Melvin Muffly wiped sweat from his presidential brow and turned to relay the command to Flint. But Flint had twisted his way past bodies hiding and bodies tied-up. Flint had left Control Central behind him.

10

No time for the luxuries of either recrimination or silent contemplation. The fat was in the nuclear fire.

"You've got to stall him now," President Muffly hissed to Cramden. "There's no choice."

Ashen-faced, Cramden picked up a communications mike from the monitor table.

"This is Lloyd Cramden," he spoke into it. "What is it you want?"

"Start the countdown immediately," Carter said. His voice was high with a strange excitement not far from madness.

"Carter, wait!" Cramden called. "We'll make a deal. We've got Trent."

"Congratulations!" Carter croaked. "But no deal. He's your problem."

Cramden beckoned to the Amazon holding Trent. She frog-marched the facsimile President to the mike.

"You've got to stop him," Cramden said, handing the instrument to Trent.

"Carter," Trent said with dignified authority, "this is your acting commander in chief. I order you to leave the capsule at once."

His laughter stopped as abruptly as it had begun.

"Acting is right," he gasped between laughs. "You're out of the cast now, Hamlet. You're expendable. Your understudy is taking over. Taking over everything. Me!"

His laughter stopped as abruptly as it had begun.

"Stop stalling, Cramden," he said in deadly seriousness. "And get on the ball. Don't waste any more time with that clown actor."

"Clown!" Now it was Trent who passed the borderlines of sanity. "You're talking to the commander of the Navy, the Army, the Air Force . . ."

Yellow-white froth flecked the corners of his mouth. Cramden yanked the mike from his hands. A husky soldier took over from the Amazon guard and pulled Trent back.

"I call upon all loyal Americans to write your Congressman!" the staggering tragedian ranted on his way out. "Picket the White House. And don't let those effeminate pinko swine fluoridate your water!" His speech ran into a wordless scream and from the scream into a babbling tirade of garbled history.

"Four-score and seven years ago!" he bleated. "You may fire when you are ready, Gridley. Millions for defense, but not one cent for tribute! Damn the torpedoes, full speed ahead! Lafayette, we are here!"

Cramden glanced to the President for guidance.

"Nothing else to do, Lloyd." The Chief Executive's shrug was all weariness.

"The countdown will begin," Cramden said into the mike.

"Good," Carter acknowledged. "Remember, should any deliberate malfunction appear on my instruments—this!" He touched the nuclear lever. "So be reasonable."

"All right," Cramden said. "Start the countdown, Captain."

The countdown officer pressed his control. Around the waiting, doom-shadowed room, technicians flipped switches, donned earphones, started their computers.

Flint had gained the vital door. It was unguarded. He raced in, giving himself a short stop to study the control panel on the wall of the first room. His mind imprinted it in detail. He left the room and went down the short hall to the Ready Room.

As he advanced he could hear monitor voices reporting launching progress and status.

"Guidance link data is complete."

He hurled himself into the Ready Room. The two

astronauts were still dazed but stirring under the eyes of two of Carter's special guards. The guards made a headlong simultaneous dive at Flint.

"Verify launch azimuth agreement."

Flint cracked their bulletheads together like walnuts and they dropped at his feet.

"Initiate power transfer."

"What the hell?" the first astronaut was asking.

"Never mind," Flint said. "I need that suit. Hurry."

While the first astronaut helped the second to shuck his suit, Flint located the wall intercom and pressed the speaker button.

"Mission Control," he called. "Mission Control."

A blue light flashed in Control Central. A technician lifted the phone below it and listened.

"It's the Ready Room, sir," he called softly to Cramden. "Flint."

"Flint!" Cramden raced to the phone.

"Sir, are you there?" Flint asked. "Good. No time for questions, sir. Get me three minutes any way you can. Three minutes!"

Flint hung up.

Cramden turned to Avery.

"It's Flint," he explained in a low voice. "He's in the Ready Room. Get him three minutes, any way you can."

"Right, sir," Avery whispered back too low for the monitor mikes to pick up.

Avery stepped up to a technician scanning a moving graph.

"You, Sergeant," he said, his wide wink invisible to Carter's connecting video eye. "Isn't that a malfunction in the tank pressure stabilization?" Avery's voice was clear now, the modulated concern of any launching official.

Flint had struggled into the space suit. Over its bulk he strapped his tuning-fork belt and tucked his lighter into an easy-access pocket.

"Good luck, sir." The two astronauts, stripped to

long johns, still made military salutes in farewell.

Flint returned the salute absently as he left for the elevator. His mind was racing too fast to hold to courtesy. The weight of the world was on his shoulders and the time he had to save it could be measured in the sweeps of a second-hand.

At every other step of the way along this perilous pilgrimage, Flint had had either some roughed out plan or some ally. In Moscow he had a general idea of what he sought and of where to find the information. Despite all the surprises of Fabulous Face, he had not gone blind into the trap. Even less than an hour ago in the Control Room, when his best scheming could find no flaw in Carter's defenses, he had had Lisa with him, complete with her Amazon regiment of concealed-weapon specialists.

Now, going into the elevator, he was alone as never before, and without any clear plan of campaign. He had always been proud of his ability to improvise, but always it had been improvisation against some framework of predictable action.

"Hold countdown." Flint treated himself to a grin of relief as the monitor technician's voice came through the speaker in the roof of the elevator. "Tank pressure stabilization is malfunctioning. Checking it out now. Hold, repeat hold for clearance."

Good old Cramden and Avery! There was a thread of time gained. It just might be enough.

But even if it were enough, Flint must face his gravest trial with nothing more to rely on than his unwritten motto: When in doubt, play it by ear.

The elevator reached the capsule. Through the thick glass Flint could see Carter suspiciously reading off the dial data from his instrument panel.

Carter made a last check, then snarled into his throat mike.

"You're stalling!" he spat. "There's nothing wrong with the tank pressure. Every register I have is apple pie, A-OK for blastoff. I'll give you ten more seconds. Ten . . . nine . . . eight . . . seven . . ."

Flint fought with the sticky slide-lock of the elevator door. His heavy gloves impeded him. In the slit between the elevator shaft and the capsule he could see a slice of blue sky.

The lock lever gave and he pushed at the door.

"Time's up!" Carter challenged from inside the capsule.

Flint swung the elevator door inward and caught the opening rings of the capsule door. Blessedly, it opened without forcing. He lowered himself into the extra capsule seat and pulled down his anchoring straps.

Carter looked across at him, fanatic eyes agleam.

"Why, it's Mr. Flint," he said from a dry throat. He let his hand down to grasp the red arming lever and its load of megaton destruction.

"I assume there's no point waiting longer," Carter said. But his hand remained still.

Cramden, Avery and the President held their breath as they watched the monitor screen in Control Central. Lisa's ladies and Flint's girls linked arms behind them in a childish reversion to a Good Luck Chain.

"This is it!" Carter rasped.

Flint adjusted his own throat mike.

"Send up the rocket," Flint said.

Cramden looked at the President.

"What choice is there?" The Chief Executive had aged ten years in the past ten minutes. "Send it up."

"Yes, sir," Cramden repeated without emotion. "Send it up, Captain."

The Control Central technicians resumed activity.

The countdown officer spoke into the television system.

"T-ten seconds, nine seconds, eight seconds, seven seconds, six seconds." He gulped and speeded the next phrases to recover the lost time. "Five seconds, four seconds, three seconds, two seconds, T-zero."

"Stage one ignition command," a second voice came from the missile silo bowels. "Eighty-seven FS one."

Red blast-off lights flashed on and off. Automatic shutter shields descended over the outer windows of the Control Room. A great shudder touched the heavy-walled structure, as if it were a glass snowstorm paper-weight being shaken by some curious, gigantic infant.

Only sporadic clicks of machinery and a soft sentence from one technician to another broke the silence of the watchful room.

The left-hand screen showed the launching pad, and the ponderous rocket rising skyward from its hard bed.

The right-hand screen framed Carter and Flint, two inhuman figures, bulging in gleaming tubular layers of space suit, both crisscrossed with their protective strapping.

On the left-hand screen the rocket belched every hue of flame from tender yellow to an iridescent purple, eating more fuel in this first effort than it would use in all the rest of its long, faster-than-sound journey. Then moving faster, ugly bulk became graceful dart as it climbed skyward.

"Stage one, all readings A-OK."

On the right-hand screen Carter and Flint lay slumped, pressed by the straining weight of their vehicle's initial thrust down into the foam of their seats, their straps as loose as untied string. A technician punched controls for a closer view. Through the masks their faces were clawed flesh over skeletal substructure. They lay on their couch seats like men long drowned and ravaged by an angry sea bent on reducing Man to some evolutionary template, crude and cruel as a primitive cave drawing yet still hinting This Is Man.

On the left-hand screen the rocket leaped into a fresh spurt of faraway exaltation. In the pale blue cloudlessness of the Caribbean sky, it was a metal bird of abstract beauty, a song of triumph against space and, in every watching mind, a monstrous lethal threat to life itself.

On the right-hand screen Carter and Flint were still recumbent, but a quick close-up showed fullness restored to their faces, eyes blinking back to consciousness never quite completely lost.

"Second-stage checking," the monitor voice reported.

Lisa clutched at Cramden's arm, awaiting the verdict.

"Second stage A-OK. All systems go."

Speech came back to Control Central. Technicians exchanged data and personal observations. The foreign scientific observers made notes.

"A perfect launch," Avery said. "Absolutely perfect!"

"For whom, Colonel?" Cramden asked levelly.

"It's still Carter's ball game, as he would say," Lisa murmured sadly.

Most of the Control Central watchers found chairs or perched on the edges of tables. The blast-off had drained its observers almost as thoroughly as the astronauts themselves. They could be seen on the monitor for a few minutes more. Then the monitor would lose contact with anything but the left-hand screen and its continuing view of the rocket in space as relayed by other tracking stations.

Flint and Carter showed equally the strain of the thrust, but both had adjusted their seats to more normal sitting posture. Both were moving their arms, leaning forward to read instruments, functioning as effectively as their splendid craft.

"Enough megatonage to destroy half the world," Cramden muttered. "And at Carter's fingertips."

"What about our interceptor missiles?" the President asked. "All those bills I signed that the slide-rule boys told me would guarantee a certain defense against nuclear attack—"

"That was assuming normal nuclear attack," Avery said.

"Only a man would use a term like *normal* nuclear attack," Elizabeth mocked.

"Let's not have childish arguments," Cramden said. "Mr. President, if we detonate that nuclear load in the atmosphere, we've had it. The whole hemisphere and far beyond."

"But we *can't* let them arm that space platform." The President grew querulous.

"It's the timing that's critical, sir," Cramden explained. "We have to wait for the last second before linking with the platform. There'll still be the hell of an explosion, but it shouldn't affect Earth."

"All right," the President said. "I understand. Have the missiles readied."

"What about Flint, sir?" Cramden asked.

"There's no choice," the President said. "Send them up."

Cramden wiped an eye surreptitiously.

"You heard the President, Lieutenant Avery," he said. "Get things moving, son."

"Yes, sir," Avery said past the lump in his own throat.

Inside the capsule, Flint and Carter had both unstrapped. Carter grinned at his unexpected traveling companion and kept his hand firmly on the red lever.

Flint found his cigarette lighter in the pocket where he had stowed it.

"Isn't the pitch and yaw indicator a little off?" he asked Carter.

As the General leaned forward to check, Flint reached into the pocket and palmed the lighter in the hand away from Carter.

"All in order," Carter growled. "You can allow a 23° variation in second stage."

They were silent for a minute.

"Or were you about to try something funny, Mr. Flint?" Carter snapped out his delayed thought.

"Funny?" Flint pondered. "I'm not the one trying anything funny, General."

"You mean I am." Carter chuckled in appreciation. "How come?"

"Just tell me one thing." Flint turned a little. "Why would anyone want to rule the world?"

"What else is there?" Carter answered with the airy indifference of full megalomania.

Now or never, Flint told himself. He flicked his left

wrist and the tiny grappling hook snaked out. The hook caught Carter's hand and lifted it by its bleeding wrist from the red lever.

Carter roared with pain. He clawed the grapple from his wrist. He reached back for the nuclear arming control, but Flint was on him like a panther, catching the bleeding hand and jerking it upward.

Both men were in prime combat condition, both trained in every special art of mayhem. They swayed back and forth in the cramped confinement of the capsule, battling life or death as they plunged past sonic speeds into space.

"Ground Control checking. Can you read me?" The capsule speaker croaked as Carter drove a knee under Flint's chin and rammed fingers at his eyes. Flint rolled away and bashed Carter's head into the instrument panel, shattering glass and knocking several hundred thousand dollars' worth of sensitive instrumentation to smithereens.

Carter recovered and took the offensive. Flint had wedged himself between Carter and the red lever. Whether he won or lost the scrap, if he could hold Carter off for another five minutes the capsule would be far enough out in space to annul immediate destruction of Earth.

"Rule!" Carter choked, slamming a foot to Flint's belly. "Rule! Power! Captain of the whole team!"

Flint twisted and rolled free, pounded two heavy punches to Carter's throat and shoved his body into a cluster of control switches under the instrument panel.

The capsule yawed and reeled in space. Carter retched, pulled himself up, located a piece of broken glass on the floor and raked at Flint's face.

In Control Central the monitor screen had gone mad, a jagged pattern of lightning zigzags alternating with blank whites and solid blacks.

"Same channel I always get at home," a Z.O.W.I.E. soldier from New Preston, Conn., remarked admiringly.

A technician dashed from his desk to confront Cramden and the President.

"Something's wrong in the capsule, sir," he said. "All our readings . . . The guidance-control system has malfunctioned and the capsule is off course. It's heading into deep space."

"It's Flint!" Cramden nearly huzzaed. "One chance in a million, but he could bring it off. Hold the interceptors, Avery."

Colonel Avery shook his head.

"It's too late, sir," he said. "They're on their way. Loaded."

Flint's girls, Lisa, Elizabeth, Helena, Simone, all looked at one another in misery. Too proud to cry, but too broken for self-control, they blinked stubbornly as salt tears marred their makeup.

In the capsule, Flint gave one tremendous karate chop at Carter's momentarily exposed neck. The mad general went down like a chopped pine, and Flint leaned against the capsule door to catch his breath.

Over the capsule intercom, he began to make out the sense of conversations picked up from the Control Central.

"It's hopeless, sir," he heard a technician's voice explaining to Cramden or to the President. "Even if the interceptors miss, the vehicle will eventually fall into the sun. They'll be incinerated."

Hair prickled at the nape of Flint's neck in ancient animal reflex to danger. He tried the capsule door and found it frozen shut.

"It's just a matter of seconds now, sir." The technician's gloomy prediction filled the whole capsule.

Flint backed across both seats and launched himself against the door. It held firm, then gave just a smidgeon. Flint braced his feet against Carter's inert body. He shoved again.

The door popped wide open, and Derek Flint was sucked dizzyingly into space.

He found himself tumbling weightlessly, his only movement the tiny contortions of his own body dwarfed by the infinity of space surrounding him. His direction —at a velocity of which he had no awareness—matched precisely that of the capsule which rocked along an arm's length from him.

But the beauties of space and the excitement of a new element shrank against his memory of the last words from the speaker: "It's just a matter of seconds now, sir."

He touched his hands to his belt and found his tuning fork. Turning his body easily, he faced the capsule and thumbed the fork. His helmetted head caught no note of the high-pitched vibration, but aimed at the capsule it repelled Flint in a flash, sending him soaring. And now he could glimpse the interceptors, gnat-sized in the immensity below.

He aimed the fork, thumbed it again, and made another leap of miles in space.

Now, looking above, he located the space platform. With proper manipulation of the tuning fork, he should be able to reach it without difficulty. This was better than skin-diving.

"A dolphin in space." He grinned inside his helmet, and thumbed the fork again.

All unaware of the capsule duel, of Flint's ejection, of tuning-fork navigation, the Control Central audience at the monitors was like a funeral congregation.

Technicians had managed to get the right-hand monitor screen into some working order again and to pick up on it the eccentrically lurching capsule, but the image was fuzzy and intermittent.

"Dammit, Avery, isn't there anything we can do?" Cramden slammed a frustrated fist into his palm.

"No, sir," Avery said. "Flint tried, a calculated risk that failed."

"Missiles into second stage. On target," the Central speaker announced with the unemotional blankness of a stationmaster calling trains.

The left-hand screen caught the precisely separated fatal beauty of the whole flight of interceptor missiles, needle-nosed destroyers hurtling uncheckable to their predestined target.

"Two seconds." Avery looked at his watch.

"I can't look!" Denise buried her head against Jan's shoulder. Jan shuddered against Terry.

There was no sound-system connection. The left-hand monitor and the right both flared into yellow-white-red explosion as the interceptors completed their mission.

The President bowed his head, his shoulders shaking with emotion. Foreign officers removed their gilt-braided caps in solemn silence broken only by sobs from every part of the room. Lisa and her steel-hard executive sisters wept openly and unashamed.

"I had no choice, Lloyd," the President said. "No choice."

"I understand, sir." Cramden gripped his Chief's arm in manly sympathy.

"He will not be forgotten," President Muffly said. "I can see at least to that. There will be a national—no, *international* day of mourning."

He squared his shoulders and swallowed a sob.

"I'd best be getting back to Washington," he said.

On his way out he stopped before the mourning knot of lovely women, Flint's girls and their recent antagonists. He struggled to think of something appropriate to say, but here all his famed political know-how left him. He could only nod silently and start to move on.

He had not yet reached the door when a new voice cut into the monitor system.

"Calling Control Central," Flint checked in. "Awaiting further instructions."

The President stopped in his tracks. Cramden did a clumsy bear-dance of joy.

"It's Flint!" he cried. "He's alive!"

Eyes sought the monitor, saw the pick-up image of the space platform, its antennae folding inward.

"He's on the platform," Cramden crowed.

"That's impossible," the President insisted.

"Of course it is, sir." Cramden was still jigging. "That's why he's Flint!"

"Three cheers and a tiger for Derek Flint!" exhorted a red-faced British lieutenant general.

The cluster of foreign military and scientific observers hip-hipped, hurrahed and roared with a will.

"Flint! Flint! Flint!"

Flint's girls, Lisa's ladies, all the Amazons fell to kissing one another and any fortunate males in the vicinity.

"Congratulations, Flint!" Cramden barked into his mike. "Now we're going to bring you home safely."

He plugged in communications connections to Z.O.W.I.E. tracking stations, took a grease pencil to the world map spread out on the main Control table.

"CYI, our Canary Islands station, shows you heading their way," he said. "We have a stand-by recovery force in that area. I'll put Lieutenant Avery on and have him give you—"

"Sorry, sir," Flint interrupted, "but the Canary Islands are a little out of the way for me. I'd appreciate instructions for landing in Central Park."

"Stubborn, wilful, undisciplined!" Cramden spoke off-mike, shaking his head with as much admiration as disapproval.

"Central Park?" he returned to Flint. "Just a minute. Captain!" he ordered a recovery officer. "Get me coordinates for Central Park."

Scratching his head, the officer rummaged through a stack of large-scale maps.

"He'll probably be home before we are!" Denise exclaimed.

"If you could make it Central Park *East,*" Flint's voice came on again. "Anywhere in the Seventies . . ."

There was a burst of static. Or was it static? Heads craned in Control Central at the almost unmistakable peals of girlish laughter filtered through the speaker cone.

"He-heh, he, ah, *nyet, Tovarich* Fleent!"

"Flint!?!" Cramden shouted. "What's going on up there? It sounds like you're not alone."

"You're right, sir," Flint spoke cheerfully. "I'm with a couple of friends."

"Flint!" Cramden tried to sound commanding. "Will you listen? You're no astronaut. You're in danger, horsing around with space hallucinations."

"That may be so, sir," Flint said respectfully, "but nothing I can't handle."

He switched off his communications mike for the moment and beckoned to the nearest of the girl cosmonauts. It was quite a cosy, if cramped, little place they had here on the platform.

She sat demurely on Flint's lap and he pressed his lips to hers.

"Kiss," Flint explained, a patient teacher.

"Kiss," she repeated dutifully. "It is so nice to be learning more the English language. More kiss, please."

"My kiss now, Anastasia." The other Russian cosmonaut tapped her buddy on the shoulder.

"Knee!" Flint pointed, rearranging his lap. "Room for everybody. Sascha kiss, then Anastasia kiss, *nyet?*"

"Da!" in chorus.

Hundreds of thousands of miles below, President Muffly was finishing his little lecture to the assembled Amazons and their leaders.

"Well, ladies," he said, "it was touch and go. I hope you've learned your lesson—that the world is better off in our hands."

Elizabeth nodded gravely.

"We realize that now, sir," she said. She waited until the President turned, then relayed a broad wink to Lisa. Lisa passed it on to Helena, Helena to Simone, Simone to Flint's girls.

The wink was recorded in no known government security-agency code book, but every girl in Control

Central could have translated it on reception into: Secret Weapons Remain the Best.

Flint, frolicking weightlessly, couldn't have agreed more.

Over Four Months on
The New York Times Bestseller List.

FUNERAL IN BERLIN

LEN DEIGHTON

A crackling tale of espionage which takes the reader from London to Prague, from a beach in Spain to the streets of Berlin. The author brings vividly to life the nightmare world of faceless men caught in the power struggles of the countries they represent.

". . . a highly readable and engaging tale . . ." —Los Angeles Times